SIX GEEZERS LYING

Six Geezers Lying

Byron James-Adams

Again thanks to my beta readers. Vic, Mel, Lil & M.D.M.
Cover Art: Canva by author.
Internal Book Design: Ingram Sparks.

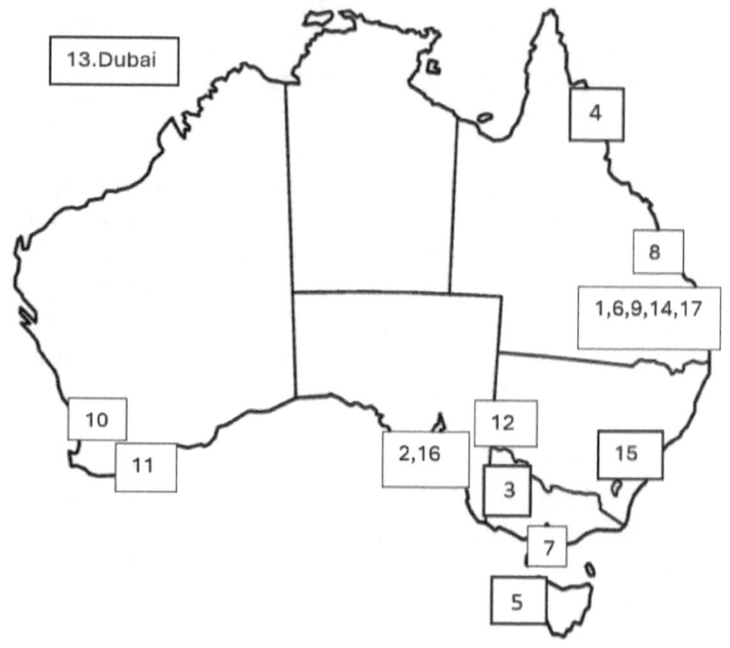

One Tricked Phoney 1. Brisbane 2. Adelaide. 3. Pinnaroo

Two Hurtled Gloves 4. Port Douglas 5. Corrina 6. Brisbane

Three French Bens 7. Melbourne 8. Rockhampton. 9. Brisbane

Four Brooding Birds 10. Perth 11. Margaret River. 12 Broken Hill

Five Moudy Bins 13. Dubai 14. Brisbane 15. Sydney

Six Geezers Lying 16. Adelaide 17. Brisbane

CHAPTER 1

Rosemary Palmer was surrounded by the sweet symphonic sounds of highly tuned engines. It was a warm, sunlit morning at the Adelaide International Raceway in the outer northern suburb of Virginia, South Australia. Puffs of blue and grey smoke swirled slowly through the throng of other car enthusiasts, but Rose was here to assist with investigating another scam. Again.

Meantime, her BFF Sandy Fraser was leaning into the engine bay of a 1976 Ford Falcon coupe, the bonnet was raised, and she was watching a Course Marshal tinker with a cable in the engine. Their friend and scam-busting associate, Nic Thorn, was sitting in the driver's seat. He called out above the din. 'I love the smell of nitromethane in the morning.'

The uniformed official stood up, nodded, gave the thumbs up, and moved away.

Sandy closed the bonnet and looked at Nic. 'What was that all about? He didn't do much apart from putting some gaffer tape over a toggle thing attached to a cable.'

Nic stepped out of the car. 'Ah, the secrets of motorsport. These races are timed events, so they turn off the line to the speedometer, which means the drivers have to go around the course without knowing what speed they are going.'

Their group looked around at the other cars undertaking the same modification in their engine bays, and Rose nodded 'I hope he knows the engine in is the back of those two beetles over there?'

Nic wobbled his head. 'Yeah, yeah, yeah…I'm sure he does, Ringo.'

Rose sighed and continued. 'If they can turn off the cable to the transmission, it prevents the mandrel from spinning, so the magnets don't rotate in the speed cup. It makes sense.'

Nic looked at her. 'Wow, I didn't realise you were a petrol-head.'

'Indeed I am, and there's still so much about me you don't know.'

Nic nodded. 'Well, welcome to The International Raceway. This is one of the only places left in Australia where we can drive really, really fast.'

Rose shook her head in dismay. 'Really, really? You told us we were here just to get smashed.' Nic smiled. 'Yep, as this racetrack is where they run the Driver Safety Courses.'

'So?'

Nic continued: 'Well, our brief is investigating an increase in motor car accident scams. It used to be fairly common, but introducing car cameras and other tracking systems has made it much harder to get away with. The fraudsters have to find smarter ways of crashing into each other, and the rumour is they have started up again somewhere here in Adelaide.'

Rose shook her head again 'You dragged Nic Thorn and Associates from sunny Brisbane just to crash someone's party here in Adelaide?'

Nic nodded. 'Yep, so we have to learn how to crash cars without getting hurt, then we have to act like we have been hurt, so we might need help to claim on the Insurance, and that's the part that hurts.'

'Which? The crashing, the acting, or claiming on the Insurance.'

'Making the insurance claim, of course, every-one knows, it's the worst part of any car accident.'

Rose shrugged and then moved over towards another car. The driver's name, "Brendan Tuttle", was emblazoned across the roof of the tiny Fiat 500CC, and with the extended wheels, it resem-bled a green turtle. The man turned off the engine, stared at the steering wheel, shaking his head, then stepped from the car and, being over two metres tall, had to fold his legs sideways to extract him-self.

Rose tried to lighten his mood. 'Hey Brendan, that's a good name on the roof. It even looks like a turtle.'

Brendan nodded and leaned in the window, pressed the horn, and it let out a long croak. Rose leaned into the car to see how small it was and noticed gaffer tape over the speedometer. 'So, they put gaffer tape over the speedo instead of the toggle on the cable?'

"Fat fingers" are the curse of anyone working on these little imps.'

'What's to stop the driver from peeling back the tape and having a peek?'

'We're all in it for fun, so there's no need to mess around with cheating. Besides, we motor racing drivers are an honest bunch. Most of us anyway, and those that aren't, drive us crazy.'

Nic ambled up. He was on his mobile phone, had a look of concern on his face and waved at Rose to listen in: 'So, Dave, what's happened to Goliath?'

Sandy moved closer, and they could both overhear the comments. 'Yep, OK, yep. I get that, too.' Nic closed the call, looked over to Rose and Sandy, and then at the little green FIAT. 'Nice car, Brendan. These two are my associates, Rose Palmer and Sandy Fraser. The three of us are here to go through the 'avoiding a crash' your team has put together. Can we start the training seminar in a couple of days?'

Brendan nodded. 'Sure, we'll meet here Thursday to run through it.'

'OK, thanks.'

There was a lull in the conversation and engine noises when an announcement was made from the race caller:

'Ladies and Gentlemen, please make your way to the start line for the next race.'

Brendan mock-saluted at Nic's group, folded himself back into the little FIAT, and started the car. It coughed and spluttered, blew out some smoke, and wobbled down the road toward the start line. Brendan leaned out the window. 'Please stay around for the race, guys; it will end in exactly fifteen minutes. This one is the best in its class.'

The little green car accelerated away, and Sandy softly jabbed Nic in the ribs. 'What's up with that, Nic? You're not racing?'

Nic smiled. 'Nope, that is something that Nic Thorn does not do. I like racing cars, but I don't like racing cars.'

Rose sighed. 'Anyway, what was the call from Dave all about? I assume it was our Dave, as in Brisbane Dave, as in our next-door neighbour looking after our Maine Coon Cat, Dave?'

Nic looked at her. 'Have you changed the name of your cat to Dave? I thought its name was Dog.' Rose punched him softly, and he continued. 'Dave was surfing the net and stumbled upon an advertisement for miniature Pekinese dogs, so he thought he'd see what they were selling for, and there was a picture of his little tea-cup dog, Goliath, and it was for sale.'

Rose nodded. 'How did he know it was his dog? All those little dogs look the same; it depends on whose handbag they are in. I've heard, the better the brand of handbag, the more pedigree in the dog.'

Nic smiled. 'Well, it wasn't so much the picture of the dog, it was more the picture of the picture. Dog was in the background of the picture of Goliath. So it's fairly obvious it was his dog.'

Sandy nodded. 'Is Dog for sale too?'

'Nope, who would want to buy an eight-kilogram cat? They tend to eat you out of house and home, then scamper over to the neighbour's place for seconds.'

Sandy nodded again 'Well, they do sell for around three thousand dollars if it's from a reputable breeder.' Nic smiled. 'Was yours?'

Sandy shrugged. 'No idea, we picked it up from Animal Rescue. However, it brought down a bank fraudster that should add to its value. It might be able to serve as a Police Cat as there are so many more opportunities for companion animals these days.'

Nic continued, 'True. Anyway, the offer price was around fifteen hundred dollars, but this is just another scam. People advertise for stuff they don't have, set up some phoney story about sending the money upfront so they can send the animal, vegetable, or mineral, whatever they are selling, and it never arrives.'

'Don't the Police get involved?'

'Not really, they are too busy putting all the human animals in jail to worry about this sort of stuff.' Rose nodded. 'So, what does Dave want you to do about it? Can you somehow look at where the website ad is coming from? Do you have access to that stuff?'

'I'll get our computer go-to guy to have a look. He can run a backwards thingy through his computer thingy and find out where the things are coming from.'

'It's good to know Chewy can step away from the dragons in his dungeon to check the real stuff, or does he still only work on your stuff?'

'He does other stuff too, you know. He doesn't sit around waiting for me to call him to look into my stuff. Sometimes he's puffed from all the stuff.'

Nic then led his little group up to the wooden bleachers to sit at the bent end of the track to watch the race start. There were at least ten starters in the first heat, including the little FIAT. It was in the rear, right behind the two VW Beetles:

'Ladies and Gentlemen, start your engines'.

CHAPTER 2

The start of the race was very underwhelming. There wasn't any tyre screeching or 'off the race line' manoeuvring, just a lot of smoke billowing from ten classic cars that were not in a hurry to get moving down the track. Most of the vehicles had headed off but in his little FIAT, Brendan was still sitting there, along with one of the VW Beetles. Rose had remained standing for the start of the race. 'Where's the need for speed, and why hasn't Brendan moved?'

'It's a time trial; he's just waiting to start. The FIAT kept stalling during his practice runs, so he's probably counting down before he takes off. The drivers have three laps to complete, and the winner is the car that gets closest to the previous three-lap trial. This time, it's all done without the speedo or having access to a timer. The Beetle might be a non-starter.'

The driver of the VW then climbed out of the car, took her helmet off, and reluctantly called the tow truck over. Rose looked down at the sad driver. 'It may have run out of Beetle juice.'

Nic grinned. 'Now, that was a great film from the late eighties, then Michael Keaton went on to be

'The Batman'. I might send up a bat signal and see what has happened.'

Rose looked at Nic. 'Do you have his number?'

'I don't think so. I don't have a bat signal either, but I might find one on Gumtree.'

Sandy sat down. 'Just tell us how this race works. Can't they use a timer on their phone or look at their watch?'

'Nope, they don't have them in the car. They can only know they are somewhere close when they go through the start line again, but their timekeepers can only raise their palms to tell the drivers to speed up or lower their palms to have them slow down.'

Nic pointed to a line of people huddled inside the fence near the starting line. 'There's Brendan's timekeeper at the end of the queue. He won't be in any hurry as Brendan has just headed off down the racetrack.' Nic turned to his phone, sent a message and a burly gentleman holding the phone timer looked at the SMS. The man danced a little jig, and Sandy recognised him or the dance move but didn't admit to which one. 'Hey, that's 'Driver'; the last time we worked with him here in Adelaide, he was invisible.'

Rose stretched out. 'Nope, that was the first time we worked with him, but the last time we didn't see him much either. He may not have been invisible, but we didn't see him.' Nic nodded, and

Rose continued: 'Will you tell us his real name, or do we keep calling him, Driver?'

'Nope, Driver, it is. Keeping my personnel safe and all that. He did marry Rita, and you know her real name. I'll have her change it if she ever works with us.'

Sandy stood up and brushed herself down. 'How come? We use our real names, and we work with you.'

'Yep, although I can come up with something else for you now if you want, guys, like Barbara Carrera and Minnie Driver.' Rose shook her head. 'Hey, they're real people. You don't use real people.' Nic shrugged.

The first lap had been completed, and the leading cars were coming through the start line. There was a lot of hand raising and lowering, and a couple of the vehicles entered Pit Lane as their timed race appeared to be over due to mechanical issues. That left only seven, but Brendan hadn't yet passed through. Around 200 metres past the start line there was a right-hand turn where the two leading cars crashed into each other, then staggered into the soft dirt and came to a dusty stop. One of the cars had done a 180°turn and was held fast against the driver's door of the other.

The hundred or so people watching stood up anxiously. The two drivers managed to climb out and made threatening gestures towards each other. One of them removed his helmet and hurled it into the ground, where it immediately rebounded and hit the other driver in the knees. The driver went down onto the ground, and she appeared to be rolling in agony, then removed her helmet and threw it towards the other driver. It missed, bounced off the side panel, and went straight back into her car through the open window. The woman driver then leant back into her car and pulled out the steering wheel as it must have detached during the crash. She threw it at the other driver. He caught it and put it into his car.

Rose looked towards the melee. 'Shouldn't someone do something? Will they come to blows?'

'I'm sure they'll sort it out between themselves. Besides, we'll catch up with them at lunch as he's the cook and she's the slicer and dicer. They run the 'Burger Veggie Van' together.'

The Safety Truck had now made its way towards the crash site, and most of the crowd had now sat back down. The two drivers still had words, and the woman had finally stood up, but the man suddenly got down on one knee and removed something from his pocket, which appeared to be a small box. Rose nodded towards them again. 'Oh no, he's not going to do that, surely? Not there...'

'What's that?'

'He's going for *the* ring....from his pocket....in the middle of a car race...that's ridiculous.'

'Hey, you never know when the big question comes, where or how.' Nic laughed at his statement, and Rose looked at him. 'Laugh it up. It should never be the right time in the middle of a car race.'

Nic shook his head. 'Well, they're a busy couple, running the Veggie Burger Van, racing the cars, and looking after their cafe. Where would you suggest? Somewhere romantic, like a walk along the River Torrens?' Rose smiled. 'Funny, Nic. I was thinking maybe a moonlight walk along one of Adelaide's beaches, then down along one of the jetties. If the answer is 'no,' he or she could jump into the water and hope that a mermaid or merman could save them.'

'Good tip for the future, Rose. Besides, I doubt it's a ring. I overheard them talking before the race, and she reminded him to ensure the new steering wheel was attached properly. The little box is most likely the steering wheel nut, and he forgot about it.'

They kept watching the driver, who had now retrieved the wheel from the other car and was chasing her partner through the dirt. She caught up with him, held the wheel over his head, and he was cowering underneath it. Then, they both burst out laughing.

Nic looked at Sandy. 'See, I told you they'd work it out. The racing drivers are a hungry lot, and they couldn't afford to give up on serving lunch.'

Their group sat back down, and Nic's phone rang and he moved away to take the call. 'Yup, what's up, Chewy?'

Sandy watched him leave. 'I hate it when he does that. It most likely means there is another caper to investigate, and we can't overhear what it is.'

Rose nodded. 'But have we ever turned one down? We get to fly around Australia, look into scams, bring down the scammers, and be home for lunch. What can be better than that?' Sandy smiled. 'Well, we've got our stuff going on. I know it's not as exciting as the Nic Thorn Investigations stuff, but it's our stuff. Does anyone need 'The She Shed' services to do home makeover stuff?'

'Oh, sorry, I forgot to tell you. I pitched an online submission to the Defence Housing Trust in Adelaide. They're starting to sell off some older properties and are looking for a team to come in and prepare them for sale.'

Sandy nodded. 'OK, we could probably handle about four or five. What numbers are they talking about?' Rose continued: 'About fifty, over two years. I went in with a high quote so that nothing may come of it.'

Sandy nodded. 'Nic probably has contacts in the Defence Services as part of his network of sticky fingers, so we might be in with a chance.'

'Yes, I know, and I should have told him about it in case he needed us to help with his stuff, but knowing what Nic knows about stuff and whom he knows, he most likely already knows, you know.'

Sandy grinned at Roses's comment as it sounded like something Nic would say. 'When will we find out?'

'Maybe next week, but seeing we are back in Adelaide, I might set up a meet and greet with the 'Heads Of, ' but I'll put twenty dollars on it that Nic already knows about.'

'Sshh, he's coming back, so we'll see what else has come up.'

Nic sat down again. 'Chewy is getting some traction with the Gumtree scam, but that's not why he rang. There's online chatter about a scam involving one of the major restaurant chains and their 'scratch and win' competition. The rumour is that someone boasts how easy it is to access the winning cards and claim the prizes. Nic Thorn and Associates have been asked to have a look.'

'So, where are we off to? Back to Brisbane, over to Perth, Sydney, or Tasmania?

'It's a national restaurant chain, Sandy, so we go where the evidence takes us. In this case, the tickets are being printed and shipped from the West Coast of the United States. '

'Woo, Hoo...California, here we come.' Sandy broke into song, stood up and started doing surfing movements... '*If everybody had an ocean....*

'Please sit down, Pit-Layne Beachley. The drivers might see you dancing and crash. Anyway, the restaurant investigation has established that the tickets are not being tampered with before they arrive, so it has to be once they hit the stores in Australia. That's where we come in, I hope you're both hungry, as we'll be eating out a lot.'

'We eat out a lot now. We've been practising all our lives to investigate this one.'

Nic nodded. 'Good point,' then pensively looked at Rose. 'When will you tell me about the Defence Homes project pitch?'

Rose handed over $20 to Sandy, and Nic noticed. 'What was that for? They only take EFTPOS here.'

'Nope, it was your last comment about the Defence Homes pitch. How much do you know?'

'Well, there were only five tenders accepted. The project would not have enough profit margin for most businesses that do that sort of thing. You'll have a twenty per cent chance of winning, but I can lower the odds if you want me to make a phone call.'

'No, but thanks for the offer. We'll see if we win on our own merits.'

'OK, but who did you put down as previous references?'

'Oh crap, I used Nic Thorn, but they won't be able to contact you to verify the details as you have that secret squirrel code of anonymity. Do pictures of you still disappear from the internet with that facial recognition thing that Chewy does?' Nic grinned. 'Yep, but the good news is I could always talk with Russell as I'm having lunch with him tomorrow.'

'Russell, who?'

'Russell Simpson, he's the Defence Housing CEO here in South Australia.'

'Damn you, Nic.'

The last of the cars was coming through the finish line, and with a well-rehearsed flourish, the marshal completed his checkered flag routine. The drivers pulled to a stop and climbed out of their vehicles, and most drivers gave a thumbs up. However, Brendan's timekeeper, Driver, was shaking his head.

In the meantime, Nic's group had made their way down to the waiting crowd and met with Driver. 'Yo, to my man Nic, and Yo to you two yo-yo's too.' Driver had held out for a fist pump but was left hanging.

Sandy looked at his timer. 'So, how did Brendan go?'

'He's about four minutes off, but this is just one of the heats, so he may be able to make it up next round.' Nic smiled. 'Does he know yet?'

'No, but they accumulate the numbers over a three-week event. The closer you can keep it to the timed trial, the more room you have for any errors.'

Nic nodded. 'Did you see the crash?'

'Yes. The nut behind the wheel wasn't bolted on.'

'That's what I heard, but they laughed it off, so that's a good thing. How scary would it have been if the steering wheel had come off? What's the maximum speed those two cars are capable of anyway?'

'About fifty in a straight line. So, no harm done, but I don't think I'll eat from their van as it might just get ugly. It's a tiny van.'

Rose nodded. 'Nic told us you got married, Driver. Congratulations.' Driver looked over to Nic. 'It was supposed to be a secret. Can't you keep a secret?'

'Sorry mate, not with matters of the heart. That is something Nic Thorn doesn't do.' A boy's voice was heard from behind them. 'Please don't do that, Mister Thorn. The group turned around, and Driver's twelve-year-old son, 'Buss', stood there smiling.

CHAPTER 3

The group of five then made their way up to Brendan's FIAT and helped him fold out of the car, and then Buss managed to sneak into the driver's seat and shut the door. 'Wow, it's so tiny here, even I can't even reach the pedals.'

Brendan leaned in the passenger window. 'The front seats have been removed, little man. I drive it from the back seat, as I'm too tall. Otherwise, my legs would have to stick out the sunroof.'

Driver smiled and looked over to Brendan. 'Do you want the good news or the bad news?'

'I don't mind. I lost my count halfway through the first lap.'

After they all sat down and ordered lunch from the Vegie Man Van, Brendan tried to coax his recent performance out of Driver. 'How did I go? Am I close?'

'Not quite, but I heard that two drivers have been disqualified as they peeked at their speed, leaving only about five others in your race. At least your odds are getting better.'

Nic's phone rang, and he saw it was Chewy.

The group watched him move away, and Driver re-started a conversation; 'Nic told me you guys are staying at the Atura Hotel by the Adelaide airport.

Sorry, I couldn't pick you up this morning. I was still in Victor Harbor dealing with my Soccer-Dad duties. The boys had a big win yesterday, and I was taking some of them home this morning.'

Sandy nodded. 'They're only just teenagers. What was their big night, too much red cordial?'

'Not quite. It was a sleepover at my place, and they binge-watched the Cars movies one, two, and three. Most of them didn't get to sleep until well after nine. It's all good, and I'm still available to drive you guys around Adelaide. Rita hasn't sold her place at Goodwood yet, so we can be based ourselves in the city for as long as needed.'

Rose nodded. 'OK, what can you tell us then? Do you know what we are here for this time?'

'Yes, something about someone crashing in on someone's party which they're not entitled to be crashing.'

Rose nodded again. 'That's about it, so given that you are already working with Brendan, is there anything we need to know about crashing his party?'

'Yes, just don't damage his FIAT as it will make him hopping mad.'

Meantime, Nic came back from his call and sat down. 'That was Chewy, and he has learned the group involved in these accident scams is setting something up this week.'

Sandy interrupted the conversation. 'How would he find that out? Surely they wouldn't advertise?'

Nic continued. 'Nope, but there is a link between the release of the latest 'Fast and Furious movies and increased chatter on the web. A small team of insurance investigators monitors that stuff, so we've been linked in to do our stuff.'

'And?'

'Well, about three groups of scammers pop their heads up, and after all that, there is a full moon this weekend too.'

Driver looked over to Brendan. 'How quickly can you get us a crash course on crashing then?'

'I can bring it forward tomorrow if I talk to the guys here. Of course, we can access cars we need to crash, but I've got to check if the Ambo's can make it.'

Rose looked at Nic. 'Do we have to have an Ambulance on stand-by?'

Nic smiled. 'Yep. Sorry, I forgot that bit. I'm nearly forty, and the old brainbox ain't what it used to be.'

'Damn you, Nic, and what's the connection to the full moon? Are we dealing with vampires and werewolves, too? Do we have to arm ourselves with a stake or a gun with silver bullets?'

Nic shook his head. 'Nope, I won't let you carry a gun. I'll Hari-Kari if you show me how, but I won't carry a gun.'

Rose looked at him. 'Hey, that's not one of yours. It sounds too clever.'

Buss piped up. 'It was the Doctor dude from that Army show. Dad's a big fan.'

Rose nodded. 'Yes, that's him. Can't you do anything original, Nic?'

'I'm the ultimate in originality; it's just that I like to copy people. The full moon means more nightlight tonight to set things up and bring things down. In the case of the motor accident scams, they won't have to use spotlights to get the best picture.'

Rose looked at him. 'Surely they don't use lighting effects. That would mean a lot of set-ups to get the best shot.'

'It's about everything. The better the quality of the car-mounted camera, the easier it is to get it past the insurance investigation. Camera's doesn't lie, you know.'

Rose shook her head this time. 'Err, I don't think so. They are still making those superhero movies in Hollywood, and I don't think they are true.'

Driver looked at them. 'Stop it, you guys. I can't keep up. So what's the plan? A stakeout at each of the locations? There's only four of us, so a solo gig is not a good idea.'

'Nope, it's a team of two at each site, three sites, so I'll need at least six. I've arranged for The Ninja Sisters, Dee-Dee and Seiko, to join us from my office in Brisbane. They'll arrive this week, and Brendan will make up the sixth.'

'Err, that makes it seven?'

'Yep, I'll put Seiko with Brendan, Dee-Dee with you. Rose and Sandy with me.'

'Are you expecting trouble?'

'No, mate, but we don't know what will happen. It's surveillance one-on-one and is likely to be as boring as question time at Parliament House, but if we bait it properly, they may turn up and make our day, or night as the case may be.'

Rose nodded. 'Does a stakeout mean we'll sit in a car with you? Why do we have to practice crashing the cars, then?'

'We'll only use the cars if it's necessary. We've only got a day to work out how to crash without being hurt, so it may be that we watch re-runs of the English cop Show, The Professionals from the late 70s. One died about seven years ago, and the other is still on TV, being a judge and a cop, gently doing deeds.'

Rose looked at him. 'Yes, please. My Father thought it was people trying to sell English Real Estate.'

Nic continued. 'Anyhow, we'll just be watching the guys that set up these types of scams; there are lots of these 'set-up' crashes on Facebook. They'll set up a crash with one person driving, then three or four others jump into the car and 'Hey Presto' everybody hurts, to quote from the American pop band R.E.M.'

'OK, we get that, but how will we intervene? Just appear from nowhere and lay down the long arm of the law. If Seiko is with us, does she have jurisdiction to make an arrest? I thought she was only a Police Constable in Brisbane. Does she carry over her gentle powers of police persuasion into other Australian states?'

'Boy, you ask a lot of questions.'

Rose grinned. 'I know, I'm like a real-life Wonder Woman as I wonder what you will get us into next. If only I had a Lasso of Truth.'

'Good point. We'll be watching from houses or conveniently placed tents. It might mean we set up a street camp and join the cardboard brigade. Here we come, North, South, East and West of Adelaide. I know we only have three groups, so I'll have to choose wisely my clever concerned cohorts.'

'When do you decide where we go? And I hope there will be soft pillows and warm blankets. It's getting cold here, and we miss the balmy Brisbane evenings.'

Brendan nodded. 'Speak for yourself, I've never ventured past the South Australian border nor had my passport stamped.'

Nic smiled. 'You don't need a passport. It's just that you can't take fruit across the border.'

The group stood up, said goodbye to Brendan, and went to Driver's car. It was a black Mercedes

Benz Van with darkened windows. Buss called out 'shot gun' and climbed into the passenger seat. Driver did all of the driver's things, checked his mirrors, checked his seat, and then grinned in the rear-vision mirror at the three passengers in the back seats.

'Where are we headed, Nic? A bit of recon before the big show?'

'Yep, but we'd better drop the little fellow home first. If we head south, we can go through Goodwood on the way. Will Rita be home?'

'Yes, her parents are staying there too, so it's all good. I'll jump on the new North-South Corridor, and we'll be back into town in less than twenty minutes.'

Nic laughed. 'Everywhere in Adelaide is under twenty minutes.'

'Hey, I live in Victor Harbor, that's more than twenty minutes from Adelaide.'

'OK, I'll give you that.' Nic nodded to Driver, cupped his hands, and held to his ears. 'Hey, little man, please watch a movie and use your headphones. We've got some secret squirrel stuff to discuss with Uncle Nic.'

'Sure thing, Dad.' The boy hooked things up, plugged things in and started watching things on his screen.

Nic waited, then began: 'OK, there are three sites we're looking at today. One at Christies Beach, then Blackwood and that multiple-circle thing they call the Britannia Roundabout at the end of Kensington Road. That covers North, South and East. At this stage, there's nothing in the west as the insurance guys reckon there are too many people around for the scammers to set something up, even in the middle of the night.'

Sandy nodded. 'I'll avoid the west, as Adelaidians like their naked midnight swims.'

Driver nodded. 'It's only at Maslin's Beach where you can go 'unclad' and about forty kilometres further south. It became the first nudist beach in Australia in nineteen seventy-five, but it's beautiful all year round, not just in summer when most people hang out. Oh, and every January it has the nude Olympics.'

Sandy continued. 'Wow, Driver, you seem to know a lot about it.'

Driver shook his head. 'No, I've never heard of it.'

CHAPTER 4

After dropping off Buss, the group drove south towards Christie's Beach. Nic handed over the dossier detailing the backgrounds of the accident scams and what they should be looking out for. It was pretty comprehensive. Rose had scanned through the pages. 'Wow, there's quite a lot going on, right? No wonder I have to pay so much for my car insurance.'

'You don't have a car.' Nic continued: 'Anyhow, I like the names they've come up with, 'Swoop and Squat', 'The Drive Down', 'The Sideswipe', but my favourite is the 'Bad Actors'.

Driver looked over at Nic. 'Wow, is that a complete list?'

Nic shrugged. 'The actors are just the 'shady helpers.' They hone in and gently persuade you to use one of their own repairers or tow truck drivers; then they take your car away, never to be seen again without paying the ransom. That's not what we think we have here, as it's likely just a straight crash and cash-in.'

Rose smiled. 'OK, what's the name given to those types of scams? 'Crash and Carry'?'

'Very good. I might use that one.'

They arrived at Christies Beach, located about twenty kilometres from the city centre and drove slowly along the main beach road, looking at the ocean on their left and the houses and buildings on the right. Sandy had lowered her window to let the warm sea breeze blow through her hair. 'What are we looking for, Nic?'

'Nothing really, just getting a vision of where everything is, where something is likely to go down, and the best place to set up camp. That sort of thing.'

Rose was already busy jotting down the local points of interest and had already flipped over to a second page. 'Well, this is a good place for something to happen. It would have to be early morning, around two or three, as too many houses around here might get woken up by the noise of a car crash. It has to be somewhere discreet. I would guess at this roundabout.'

Nic looked over and smiled. 'I have taught you well, but why this spot then?'

Driver pulled the car to a stop in the car park. They looked about, and Rose read from her notes: 'It's the event's timing. A bright street light on the end of the streets and good vision up and down the esplanade. If they miss-time their approach, there's plenty of runoff to enter into the car park for a re-start if needed.'

Driver agreed: 'I would say she's right, Nic, and this is one of those notorious 'black spots' the Department of Main Roads are arguing about. You think they'd just put in a set of traffic lights and force people to stop.'

Nic grinned. 'People don't always obey traffic lights, especially the scammers, but you're correct, as most car accidents involving roundabouts hardly ever result in deaths. It's not hard to negotiate one; remember to give way to your right.'

Driver continued: 'Yes, and there's a lot of oblivious drivers thinking they are the only ones on the road, or that might is right, or just being on the road means they're right.'

Nic took one last look around and they headed back to the van. 'Right then, it's time we left and headed up to the Britannia Roundabout. Now, that's a roundabout worth writing home about. It's the busiest in Adelaide and the most complex.'

Driver nodded. 'I know it well. I liked it so much better before they changed it about seven years ago, but you can't stop progress or slow-gress, as it's a nightmare to negotiate. Have a look at the website they posted when it was altered. Even that doesn't make sense as the cars magically jump lanes without indicating.'

Nic replied. 'I know, but at least the number of crashes has reduced as people now avoid it entirely.'

Sandy nodded this time. 'My Dad avoids it, too. He's recently moved into a suburb nearby, which means going through it if he drives into the city.

He finds walking past it much safer, so he sets himself up with a chair and thermos full of coffee to enjoy all the car crash craziness. He reckons there's a good chance they'll put in traffic lights. Eventually.'

They drove along Fullarton Road, Dulwich, and pulled into a small car park just before the Britannia roundabout. Rose hadn't seen the site before and was reading from her phone while scribbling down more details in her notebook: 'According to the website, over fifty thousand cars go through this roundabout daily. Hang on, that was about five years ago, so I assume we can add another ten or twenty thousand cars.'

Driver was mesmerised by the meandering madness, then turned back to her. 'I don't think so; fewer people have relocated to Adelaide in the last five years. Most of them have given up trying to work out how to live around here and have settled near a beach where it's much safer. It's too expensive this side of Adelaide city anyway, and the average home is pushing over two million dollars.'

A car horn blared followed by a screeching of brakes, which broke the group from their trances. Two drivers had stopped in the traffic and began rudely gesturing to each other about who had the right of way. This held up the rest of the vehicles coming into the roundabout, and then a cacophony of car horns started.

Sandy had to yell to be heard. 'SO, YOU RECKON THEY'RE GOING TO STAGE A CRASH HERE?'

Nic called out: 'YEP. IT GETS MUCH QUIETER WHEN IT'S TWO O'CLOCK IN THE MORNING WHEN THE REVELLERS LEAVE THE CBD AND HEAD HOME.'

The 'accident' drivers finally decided to move on, much to the other frustrated drivers' delight. Sandy continued: 'This road heads to the Eastern Suburbs and eventually up to Penfolds Winery at Magill, so I don't think many late-night revellers live over this way. Most of them would be well and truly home and in bed by then.'

Nic smiled. 'Sandy, where's your spirit of adventure? We're in Adelaide, and there's a bottle shop behind the nearest Hotel and a Church on every corner. You can repent your sins, re-fill, and then re-start the re-revelling.'

'I don't think so. Besides, will this road junction ever get quiet enough to stage anything smashy?'

Rose interjected. 'It's ideal for fast-moving, in and out. If they wanted to stage a crash, it would happen quickly, and there are plenty of places to wait and then jump into a car. Or the car can drive into the vegetation in the middle, then add in a couple of 'casualties' and 'witnesses' as they arrive.'

'You have it all planned out, don't you?'

'Yes, and as the Britannia Hotel is on the corner over there. I call dibs for Sandy and me to do our surveillance from here. Are you with us, Nic?'

'Our last site to visit is at Blackwood, and yes, it's in the Adelaide hills, and it will most likely be cold ......I agree... I also call 'dibs' on this site, but it's my show, so I don't have to call 'dibs''.

They all nodded in agreement and returned to the car to head to the next site at Blackwood. Driver drove into a small shopping centre, and they all looked around. 'Nic, it's well after two p.m. Can we stop for lunch yet? How long will it take for us to get back?'

Nic looked at them. 'Have a guess.'

They entered the local chocolate café, and Sandy smiled. 'Hey Nic, this is the same specialty franchise store as the one we went to last time we were in Adelaide. I bet they serve a great chai latte.'

'Yep, they do, Sandy, and as Rose has always said: 'When in doubt, go to chocolate.'

They ordered meals and chose a table, looking straight out at a roundabout. It was much less busy than the one by the Britannia Hotel but just as frenetic. Rose stood up, moved closer to the window, cupped her hands against her face, and stared out. 'This site is too dark, Nic. Here, it is just after noon, and buildings shade it. They'll need to set up lights to get a clear vision for the car cameras.'

'My thoughts, too, but there's still a chance they could rig something up. It will be cold up here, though, and there's nowhere to set up unless we can stay in this café. I think they shut at five p.m., so I'll see if I can get their OK to do our surveillance from in here.'

Rose looked at him. 'Why would they do that? And how do you do that? You're not with the Police. Do I have to hand over a warrant or something?'

'Nope, I don't know yet, but I'll set up Seiko and Brendan in here, and that might be intimidating enough for the owners to believe we are doing something legitimate.'

Driver smiled. 'Yes, Brendan, the bean pole, and Seiko, a Ninja Police Officer, I'd be scared.'

Nic moved away from the table, asked to see the Store Manager, and returned after less than two minutes. 'They agreed to let us do it as long as we don't damage anything.'

Rose looked up. 'That was quick.'

'Yep, I thought I'd recognised her, then realised she was holding the steering wheel over her husband's head earlier today. We were chatting about the whole 'nut behind the wheel' thing, and then Toby came out from the kitchen.'

Toby and his partner sat down with Nic's group. 'So, you want to set up a surveillance thing in our little café just in case you see someone doing something to do with a staged crash?'

Nic nodded. 'Yep. Please, if we may, and that's about the extent of what you need to know about it. The less you know, the more you need to know that you shouldn't know.'

Toby looked over to his wife, then back to Nic. 'OK, tell us what you need.'

Nic nodded. 'I'll have two of my guys sitting in here watching the roundabout. I'll give you a call when we are ready.' They both nodded.

Nic settled the bill, and the group went outside to the car. They climbed in Driver turned around. 'What just happened?'

'Networks, work, Driver. It's all about finding people that work in your network, then you can add them to your network, but be careful if you don't want them to network your network, as that becomes lots of work.'

Sandy laughed. 'Just how do you keep it all together?'

'I have no idea, and that's all you need to know to keep me sane.'

'Thanks. So, where are we off to now?'

'To the Hotel where it's a bit warmer.'

CHAPTER 5

When Driver dropped the group back at the airport hotel Seiko and Dee-Dee were waiting in the foyer. They both nodded hello to Sandy and Rose and hugged Nic. Dee-Dee took the lead. 'Hi Nic, we caught an earlier flight from Brisbane and saved two hundred dollars.'

'Sure, but it costs two hundred dollars a night to stay here, so unless you plan to sleep on a beach somewhere, welcome to the Atura. Have you arranged a room?'

'Not yet, but now that you're here, can we join in on the car crashing course on Friday then?'

'Sure, but I have good and bad news. The course has been brought forward to tomorrow, pending the Ambulance guys being available.'

Seiko nodded. 'So, is that the good news or the bad news?'

'Well, it depends on your perspective. We've just visited the sites where we think the car accident scam may happen, and you drew the beach. Seiko, unfortunately, you got the overnight at a café in Blackwood.'

'That doesn't sound too bad. Whom am I bunking with?'

'Well, I'm with Rose and Sandy at the Britannia Hotel, but there's no accommodation there. I haven't quite worked out how it's going to work. Maybe we work on drinking lots of coffee and staying awake for the duration.'

Seiko nodded. 'So, am I with Driver, or Brendan, the other driver?'

'You're with Brendan. I'll have three camp beds, but we'll set that up tomorrow night under the guise of a stock delivery to the café.'

'Three beds? Who's the third one for?'

'For Brendan's legs; otherwise, they'll hang off the end.' Nic then stood up and directed the group to a Private Room so they could run through the details: 'Ok, guys, whatever this is, we don't know if it will happen over the weekend, but the Insurance Investigator Team is pretty sure something will happen. One of the main guys involved has just purchased the latest Toyota Supra for around ninety thousand dollars. That doesn't mean much, but he hasn't been able to sell his current car.

Rose nodded. "Was it a Mitsubishi Lancer EVO or Subaru Impreza, and he's trying to upgrade?'

'Nope, it was just a Holden sedan. Apart from selling parts, he couldn't do anything else with it. It was the best of a bad bunch.'

'Why has he come to our attention?'

'He's part of a posse involved in illegal streetcar racing. Unless he's going straight, he'll likely be involved somehow. Somewhere on his horizon is the lure of a nasty accident and a nice compensation claim.'

Seiko addressed the group. 'Yes, and the latest Fast & Furious promotion is starting to show on-line, which includes a Toyota Supra, so it's come to my people's attention too. All these car movies give the young guys the enthusiasm to be driving heroes.'

Rose nodded. 'Those shows have certainly raised the profile of classic cars, too. They've used early seventies model Dodge Charges, Chevrolets, and lots of Nissans. About eighty cars were destroyed in the first movie, and over two hundred in the Tokyo Drift one. What a waste.' Rose then looked at Nic. 'Now that's pop-culture trivia worth knowing.'

Nic laughed. 'So, Rose, have you filled up your notebook yet?'

Rose went to respond when her phone rang, so she moved away to take the call. Nic watched her go. 'I hate it when she does that; how do I know what she's getting me into.'

Rose returned after about ten minutes. 'So Nic, when were you going to tell me I'm your + 1 at the Adelaide Convention Centre on the future direction of Defence Housing in South Australia? They rang me to check if I had any special dietary needs.'

'Oops, sorry.' He looked over to Sandy. 'Would you like to be a +1 at lunch tomorrow too?'

Sandy looked at him. 'A +1 can't be a +2, as the numbers won't add up.'

'Well, Russell needs a +1 as his partner has decided to play golf instead, and having a spare chair at the presenter's table makes it look a little empty.'

'Wow, thanks for that, being a late substitute and all. We have nothing to wear, so we have to go shopping. Have we got time to get to the Burnside Shopping Centre? It's the only place in Adelaide where we can find the stuff that Rose and I like to be seen in if we're to be seen in Adelaide.'

Seiko shook her head, then looked at Nic. 'Aren't you forgetting something?'

'Sorry, Seiko and Dee-Dee, there's only room for two +1s at the table.'

'Nope, you dope. You're trying to bring the crashing car course to tomorrow, so if that happens, none of you will attend the lunch.'

'Oh crap, I forgot. I'm getting too old for this stuff.'

Nic stood up and left the room, and they assumed he was calling Brendan to ensure the course would happen tomorrow. He returned a couple of minutes later.

Driver looked up. 'How did it go?'

'Yep, all good. The driving course only lasts for three hours. One hour learning how to crash, and the second two listening to how to avoid them. We've got an Ambulance on standby, and the Fire

Brigade guys will be there just in case.' Sandy stood up and stretched. 'Woo Hoo, we might just need to be helped out of the crashes by the hunky men in uniform.'

'I don't think so, Sandy. We won't have time as we'll be too busy studying.'

Nic arranged for the Ninja sisters to check into the Atura, and they agreed to meet in the Hangar Bar and Grill at 7 p.m. to discuss the finer points of crashing someone's party.

Nic was satisfied they could talk freely as only three other tables were occupied: 'Guys, it could get boring as it may not happen on Sunday morning. There's no evidence this group will make it happen, but the Insurance Investigator Team is happy with what we have put together so far, and we are good to go whatever happens.'

Seiko leaned in. 'I still don't get it. Why aren't they putting their people into this?'

'It's about outsourcing. The Insurance people have to answer to other Insurance people higher up the totem pole, so if they can bring us in on the ground, they don't have to worry about things that may or may not happen in the air whilst they've got their heads in the sand. They have to justify the expense.'

'We are the expense?'

'Yep, so that's why we've been brought in. I agreed to set a fixed fee that's in line with what's reasonable. At this stage, there's enough in the budget for three teams to watch the three sites for a few days, but if we have to go longer, I might have to change things.'

'And send us some of us back home to Brisbane?'

'Yep, Driver lives here, so I might have to scale down to a one-person team.'

'And a Rock, Paper, Scissors competition to determine who stays?'

'Nope. I'll stay here in Adelaide, all by myself.' He broke into song: *'Don't wanna be, all by myself, anymore...'* then looked over to Rose. 'That's a Celine Dion song.'

'Maybe, but a dude called Eric Carmen did it first, but then again, he stole it from Rachmaninoff's Piano Concerto No 2, in C Minor.'

They all looked at her. 'It was a Trivial Pursuit question.'

'Really?'

'No, Nic. Anyhow, my Father is running an Art Show in Brisbane in a couple of months, and his painting will be on display.'

'But it's a fake, Rose.'

'Yes, and it's on display as a fully declared a fake, but apparently, other genuine paintings will be for sale.'

Nic looked at her. 'Apparently?'

Rose continued: 'Well, we will ask him about that. I've tried researching the Art Foundation that's operating the Art Show. It's an impressive website, but the geezers lying behind it could be passing off fake art.'

'So, you'd like Nic Thorn and Associates to looking into that'

'Yes, if we can, maybe after this Adelaide thing ends. The show is not until April first, so we have some time.'

Seiko nodded. 'That's April Fool's Day, Rose.'

'I know. I hope my Father knows what he is doing.'

'OK, I'll get Chewy to do some background checks. What is the name of the Foundation?'

'It Keeps Changing.'

'OK, even if it does, Chewy can find something on it. What is its name now?'

Rose shook her head. ''It Keeps Changing'. That's the name of it. It wouldn't surprise me that one of the old dudes involved in the Art Foundation has a quirky sense of humour.'

'Gee, you're one suspicious rose, Rose.'

'I've learned from the best.'

Nic smiled. 'Hey, that's not fair. I've worn out many shoes shuffling around Australia looking for clues.'

Driver laughed. 'You wear rubber-soled shoes that don't wear out in a hurry.'

Nic looked around for the waiter. 'Yep, that is true. How long does filling our drinks order and making my chai latte take?'

The waiter suddenly appeared. 'Sorry to have kept you waiting, Sir. We do have other patrons.'

Sandy looked around but couldn't see anyone else, and the waiter noticed. 'We had an order for a chai latte, and my barista had to Google how to make it.'

As it was nearing 10 p.m. and they were all in their rooms, however Driver had gone to the van to make sure it was locked. He returned the reception area and called Nic's room. 'There's something you need to see at the car. It looks like it's been attacked by a Godzilla want-to-be.'

'Stay there, and I'll come down.'

Nic called Seiko's room and asked that she put her 'I'm with The Police' game face on just in case it was needed. Unfortunately, Dee-Dee overheard, and as they were next to Rose and Sandy's room, Rose heard the commotion and joined them in the corridor.

They all met with Driver downstairs and he led them to the car. It was as he had described it: most panels were damaged, the headlights were smashed, and even the sunroof had been peeled back.

'I don't think I'll drive it home, so I'll call a taxi.'

Seiko wandered around the car, wrote a few lines in a notebook, and tucked it into her back pocket. 'This is not good, Nic. Do you think the Insurance scammers could be onto us already?'

'Maybe, but before we jump to conclusions, how about I look at the film from the Closed Circuit cameras? I'll report it to the Airport Security people, and they should be able to give me access to the vision, but firstly, let's get Driver home safe tonight.'

The group waited with Driver as Nic went off to call Airport Security, and a couple of minutes later, Nic returned. 'Well, that was interesting. The guy who answered the phone told me it's their utmost responsibility to ensure the safety and protection of any assets during your stay. He also told me to have a nice day.'

Rose looked at him. 'Didn't that sound a tad rehearsed?'

'So, I hung up and called him again, and do you know what he said?'

'The same thing? And let me guess; the office was closed?'

'Yep, so I'll check it out in the morning. The car isn't going anywhere tonight. Driver will organise another one and pick us all up in the morning at nine for a catch-up with the Insurance people. So it's goodnight from me and good night from him.'

Sandy looked at him. 'That's from the Two Ronnies. They were English comedians, but it's not that funny anymore. Give me Rowan Atkinson any day.'

CHAPTER 6

Driver met the group in the foyer in the morning, and they waited for Nic. They were worried as he was never late and assumed he was with the Hotel Security people. Nic arrived and apologised: 'I'm sorry, I slept in. The bed was so soft, and don't get me started about the pillows. I forgot about the important stuff we were doing, is that enough stuff for you all to believe me?'

Rose looked at him suspiciously. 'If you think we're going to be fooled by all that stuff, you can get stuffed.'

'That's not nice, Rose. Anyway, I've already had my chai latte and found out what happened to the car, too.'

Sandy nodded. 'You must have been up early then?'

'Yep, I was up with the early birds. I met with the Security people at six. We went through the vision, and it turned out it was just a couple of well-heeled kids looking for a place to sleep. They tried to break into the car, arguing about who was doing the most damage. It escalated from there. They even stole the Mercedes Benz emblem from the bonnet. Who would do that?'

Rose piped up. 'A Mercedes Benz emblem collector. Did they catch them?'

'Nope. It turned out the security patrol team were a couple of guys down, and their rounds weren't completed properly.'

Seiko looked at him suspiciously. 'It doesn't make sense. The damage didn't look like it was random. It was too contrived and felt personal. Is there something you're not telling us?'

'Sorry guys, F.M.E.O.'

Sandy looked at him. 'Don't you mean FOMO? The Fear Of Missing Out?'

Rose realised what Nic had meant by the acronym and addressed the group: 'It means 'For My Eyes Only.' I assume there would be more to the vision, but Nic doesn't want us to know.'

Nic nodded and tapped the side of his nose with his forefinger. 'Yep, it's a case that only Nic needs to know, but I will tell you this, someone knows something is up.'

When they arrived at the International Raceway, a security guard met them at the entrance gate and directed them to the seminar rooms where Brendan was waiting.

'Thanks for coming; this will be an experience I hope you'll never have to experience. We have set up a few scenarios where you will be involved in a car crash, learn how to avoid being involved in a car crash, and afterwards, we can all crash at my place for drinks.'

Nic nodded. 'Have you got the Ambulance and Fire Brigade on stand-by?'

'Yes, but they shouldn't be needed as the training is initially with a car on a pneumatic hoist and an enjoyable movie. It's a simulator.'

Rose laughed, and Sandy objected. 'Damn, I was looking forward to talking fiery stuff to a real Fireman or crashy stuff to a real Amboman.'

'It's all good as they look very real on the screen, and you can talk to them, but they just won't answer back. Don't worry, there are outside crashes too, but once we crash those cars, it's not a matter of 'Control, Alt, and Delete.' They don't re-set that easily, so we'll practice in here before the real thing.'

Both Dee-Dee and Seiko nodded. 'We've done defence driving courses in Brisbane, so can we look more into the background of the suspects instead?' Driver looked over to them. 'Hey, I do them every six months to keep my skill levels up too. You never know when you must drive to the best of your capabilities.'

Nic nodded. 'OK then, guys, let's just run through this now, but after the training sessions, we've set up a car for each of us to drive, and there's an awesome stereo system in them just in case you need some inspiration, and I've taken the liberty of preparing your music, and he broke into song...Rose shook her head. 'Please stop singing.

Are we going around the racetrack trying to avoid each other?'

'No, but yep. If we survive the race, it's a smash-up derby at the end, just in case you get bored.' Brendan introduced the rest of his team. They were shown to their seats and he explained the driving and crashing cars.

Nic's phone rang to the tune of 'Batman' – from the 60's TV show. 'Sorry, Brendan, it's from the Insurance Team; something must have happened.' Nic took the call and left the room whilst Brendan helped the others to log in to their allocated computers. 'OK, ladies and gentlemen, as they say, start your search engines.'

The screens opened, and a visual display system showed the statistics of car crash injuries, and deaths, and detailed how much it cost the Australian Health Industry. Then it got really dull.

Brendan went through the numbers, threw a couple of spot tests at them to make sure they were paying attention, and after about forty minutes, he hit a kill switch, and the computers shut down. Nic had not yet returned.

'OK, that ends the computer stuff, and don't worry, you'll get a Certificate of Attendance to hang on your wall, along with your posters of Daniel Riccardo.'

Rose looked at him. 'I'm more a Mark Webber fan. What now?'

Brendan rubbed his hands together. 'Now we go driving in the simulator, so strap on your seat belts.'

Sandy was the first to get settled into the simulator. A whole body 'G-suit' had been provided, including moulding to assist in controlling the muscle strain, a helmet with a 3D set of eyewear and a built-in microphone. Sandy looked the part of a professional driver and made herself comfortable with the 180° screened vision of a real race-track.

The scene re-booted, and Sandy stared down the Adelaide International Raceway race track. 'Wow, great vision. Can I stare down at the other drivers or annoy them by poking my tongue at them?'

'Do it and see what happens.' So she did, and an announcement came through her headset: *'Please keep all body parts inside the vehicle at all times.'* The group laughed, and the system began as the car raised itself on the hydraulic hoists in readiness for the race simulation.

Brendan donned his set of headphones and spoke into a microphone. 'Are you ready to go, Sandy? The car drives like a normal one, so you will have to change gears and operate the clutch. It's not a racing gear change system per se, but you can 'red line' the rev counter before you change if you want to.'

Sandy nodded, so Brendan continued: 'One last thing. Did you have a big breakfast this morning? The sim accelerates and brakes aggressively, so you might pull a few 'G's if you take corners too fast. It's about the same muscle strain as a roller-coaster, so you might sometimes feel a bit queasy. Watch out for the other cars around you; they will be overtaking and braking, too.'

Sandy nodded. 'Anything else I need to know?'

'Nope, take it easy on the first lap. Just get an understanding of how the car handles and the track. It's not a competition. Three laps in total, then we swap to someone else. Have fun.'

Sandy gave the double thumbs up and smiled at him, and Brendan moved over to one of the tables and grabbed an empty bucket.

Rose looked at it, then at him. 'What's that for?'

'If Sandy drives it hard, by the second lap, she'll be feeling the change in the performance and might get a physical reaction. This is to allow for it.'

Sandy was a competent driver and, by the end of the first lap, was pushing the car reasonably hard down the straight, and at the end, as there was a right-hand turn, they watched the car brake heavily. The simulator lurched and settled down again. There was a camera in the car directed towards the driver, and the strain was beginning to show on her face as Sandy started taking deep breaths.

Rose was a little concerned. 'Err, Brendan, I think she might be feeling the effects, or is it the green colour of the duco?'

'Oh no, that's all her.'

Suddenly, the car stopped, and Sandy managed to take off her helmet just before she vomited over the vehicle's console. The others watched the drama unfold on the TV screen. Brendan called out. 'Damn.'

'What? Does that happen often?'

'Yes, but I wasn't quick enough with the bucket.'

Meantime, Nic had finally returned and nodded towards the car simulator. 'It looks like you were too late with the bucket, Brendan.'

Brendan nodded. 'And that ends the lessons for today.'

Dee-Dee, Seiko and Rose smiled, and Brendan assisted Sandy to exit the vehicle whilst his other team members began the process of deep cleaning the inside of the car.

Sandy stood still and allowed Rose to sponge the residue from the driver's suit. 'I'm sorry, Brendan, I pushed it too hard.'

'No harm done, but I can't certify that the others have completed their race induction, so we won't be able to drive the real cars around the track.'

Nic nodded. 'It's all good as things have changed a bit anyway. I've been on the phone with Chewy, and apart from getting more traction on the

'Gumtree' thing, we've been advised that we won't need to camp out at the roundabouts.'

Driver looked at him. 'Have they pulled Nic Thorn and Associates off the case already?'

Nic shook his head. 'On the contrary, it all went off early, and they crashed their party.'

Rose nodded. 'When?'

'Last night, well actually early this morning. We had the right place but the wrong time. The investigators have asked us to take a look this afternoon.'

'Where?' It was Dee-Dee this time.

Nic continued: 'At the Britannia roundabout. We're going to meet them at two o'clock. The car is yet to be removed. They are re-directing traffic via detours, and people are getting a little annoyed.'

Brendan nodded. 'Well, we can't do anything more here now due to Sandy's sudden expulsion of excitement. You guys are free to go if you like. Otherwise, we can listen to the music selection that Nic put together for the race.'

They all looked at him, but Rose responded. 'No, but thanks anyway, Brendan. We can race back to the Hotel, though.'

CHAPTER 7

After dropping Sandy back at the Atura Hotel to freshen up and recuperate, the rest of the group drove to the Britannia Hotel. They ordered lunch and sat in the alfresco area overlooking the mayhem at the roundabout.

Earlier in the day, the police had cordoned off the crash site and split the traffic lanes to allow the cars travelling south to north to traverse the roundabout on the right-hand side, but those travelling east to west were on their own. It was a good idea in theory. However, anyone who wanted to go left towards the city had to make a second circuit, and remnants of toppled plastic traffic cones were strewn across the road.

The Police had long since left, and there were now three 'lollipop' traffic attendants trying to control the traffic with stop-go signs. They were too far apart, had no communication radios, and relied on waving hands to make their directions understood. It wasn't working, and some vehicles were doing their own thing by simply driving over the middle of the dual roundabouts to escape the chaos.

Finally, Seiko and Dee-Dee had had enough and moved to the area to assist, and Seiko flashed her

Police Badge to convince the traffic attendants to resume the normal flow direction. Cones were collected, and the traffic started moving again, albeit slowly and carefully.

Meantime, Nic and Rose had carefully sashayed through the traffic and met with the two Accident Investigators in the middle of the roundabout. In an early model, Holden Camira was precariously resting on a broken tree stump. The car was substantially damaged, and so was the surrounding foliage. There was also evidence of a grass fire, but no evidence of a second vehicle being involved.

Nic leaned forward. 'So what time did this happen?' One of the Investigators looked over at him. 'I assume you're the OGREs?'

Nic leaned towards Rose. 'Observe, Gather, Report and Evaluate.'

Rose nodded, and the Investigator continued: 'Around three in the morning, there were no witnesses, and three people were taken to hospital. It was a mess, two cars involved. Six casualties. The tow truck has already decided it's a crane job, so we have to wait until tomorrow morning to remove the car.'

Rose put her hands in her pockets and looked at the scene. 'What happened to the second car?'

The man looked at her. 'Who are you?'

'Rose Palmer. I'm with Nic Thorn and Associates. I guess I'm an O.G.R.E, too.'

'OK, I'm Jay, but they call me 'Soop', and that's Penn Brophy taking the pictures of the car.' Penn carefully put the camera on the ground, walked over and shook hands with them. 'It drove away, but the occupants presented themselves to Emergency at the Royal Adelaide Hospital. They didn't wait for an Ambulance. The three occupants of this car were extracted from the vehicle by the Fire Brigade boys and then taken in Ambulances to the hospital. They're still in there pending further medical examinations. The driver is in an induced coma.'

'Are they in isolation or together in the same ward?'

'It's a public hospital, so most likely the same room.'

Rose whispered to Nic. 'Working on their stories, I bet.'

The second investigator overheard the comment and looked at Rose, but Nic responded instead. 'Rose, we don't know anything about anything yet, so let's not make something of nothing until we've looked at everything. That's why the experts are here.'

Soop then did a twirly thing with his forefinger, indicating they had gathered enough evidence, and he nodded to Nic. 'So, do you guys want to make any comments?'

Rose retrieved a small book from her back pocket, re-read some of her notes, and looked down the road at where the car must have come from. 'There are no fresh skid marks I can see, so how did they come together?'

'We don't know yet, Ms Palmer, as the patients haven't been interviewed. We're heading there now if you'd both like to come along.'

Rose continued. 'Sure, that would be good, thanks. I doubt it was a 'T-bone' collision as the second car couldn't have been driven away after the accident, and this car seems to be very high up against the tree trunk, too. It's almost as if it was dragged or pulled up there rather than driven into it. Do you mind if I climb on top of the car and take a look?'

They looked at Nic, and Soop nodded.

Nic helped Rose to climb onto the bonnet, and she looked around. There was a solid tree trunk to the left of the car. 'I've got some damage up here in the fork of the boughs. It's too high to have been caused by the car, and it looks like a chain or something stronger was threaded through here. I'll take some pictures with my phone.'

After spending a few minutes on the bonnet, Rose carefully pivoted and returned to Nic. 'These older cars have a hook under the bumper. I'll check for abrasion marks.' Rose took a look, took a couple more photos, and stood up. 'Now that's interesting; you'd think if the car hit the tree, there would be more damage to the underside of the car.'

'How long has Ms Palmer been doing this stuff?'

Nic smiled. 'About three years with me, but before that, she was a spy for ASIO.'

Rose put her notebook in her pocket. 'I was not. I like cars and know some stuff about them, but I use the experts when needed. It's good to bring in an expert, as they might teach you something that looks like nothing means something.'

Nic smiled at Rose. 'You're only new to all this soft shoe shuffling stuff, and we talk the same investigative lingo littered with confusion and obfuscation.'

The group returned through the traffic and into the Britannia Hotel for a well-earned drink. The seven gathered some tables together and started going through the brief.

Driver stood up. 'I'll get some drinks organised. Name your poison, they have many beers on tap here.'

Nic nodded. 'I'll just have sparkling water, thanks, Driver – stirred, not shaken.'

The rest of the group spoke up, too. 'Make mine water too, please.'

'Wow, that's a cheap round; thanks, guys.'

Dee-Dee returned from taking a phone call and was smiling. 'Hey Nic, if we all go to the hospital, the patients might get slightly spooked. So, can Seiko and I take the afternoon off?'

'Sure, but I didn't think the Ninja Sisters were into shopping. Rose and I can get an Uber to the hospital, and I'm sure Driver will be happy to help you shop to you drop.' Meantime Driver came back with three bottles of Mt Lofty Sparkling Spring Water. 'I'm doing what now?'

'Taking Seiko and Dee-Dee shopping.' Driver stifled a laugh, then looked at Nic. 'Mate, they're going skydiving out at Lower Light. I'll take them out there, and we'll meet you back at the Hotel at about six. If that's OK.'

'Yep, I should have said drop until you stop.' Nic laughed at his statement, but the others didn't. They finished the drinks, and then Dee-Dee, Seiko, and Driver left. Nic organised the Uber to the hospital.

When Rose and Nic arrived at the hospital, the two Investigators were already there along with one of the Ambulance Officers who had attended the early morning incident. They were ushered into an office, where a Doctor and an ER Nurse were waiting.

The Doctor was reviewing the patient's charts when they entered. 'Wow, it takes five of you to investigate this one?' The Ambulance Officer nodded. 'So Doc, any prelim results that seem a little odd?'

'Well, we've managed to get the driver out of the coma. He was unconscious when he arrived, but it was more to do with a dose of propofol than the accident. He must have been injected soon after the crash. If that's the case, this is one of the worst staged crashes I've seen.

Both Soop and Penn nodded. 'So, what made you think it was staged?'

The Doctor continued. 'Well, apart from the traces of the drug in the driver's system, the passenger has a rash on his face and hands. It looked like hives; then his lips started to swell. He's also got a round welt mark on his right hand from something he must have picked up somewhere. A symbol is etched into his palm, surrounded by a ring about the size of a teacup. It would have hurt, so we've mainly focussed on that injury. We took photos of it, and they're in the file.'

The ER Nurse added. 'I tried to convince him that if no drugs were involved, he would be fine to go home today, but then the patient started to cry.'

'So, the truth came out?'

'Nope, he just kept crying, so we shot him with a dose of sleepy stuff to send him off to La La Land.'

'And the rash?'

'Propofol can do that if you are allergic.'

Nic nodded. 'Sorry Doc, can I ask what happened to the third person in the car and the other car's occupants?'

The Doctor smiled. 'She's already been discharged and was collected early this morning. We didn't get many details, and I believe her name was fictitious. No I.D. either, so her name is all we have. The other car drove away, leaving the three in the smashed car.'

'OK then. The young woman...what name did she use?'

'Isabella Swan.'

Rose laughed. 'I see what you mean, and were the two others, Edward C and Jacob B?'

Nic looked over at her. 'What's that from?'

The Doctor crossed his arms and put the reports down on the desk. 'The lady knows her pop culture. The name is from 'The Twilight' series, so as it's turned out, these guys might just be a real pain in the neck for wasting our time.'

Rose nodded. 'Definitely staged then?'

'I don't know. It's my job to fix them up so they can live their normal lives, whatever that is these days, and on that note, I will bid you farewell.'

The Doctor handed them a copy of the results and then left the room with the ER Nurse and Ambulance Officer. Nic opened the evidence dossier, dropped the medical reports inside, and moved to the Investigator's iPad so they could review the downloaded .jpeg files of the accident site. Rose had already sent them the ones that she had taken.

'There's something I don't get here. I counted at least five traffic cameras at the site when we were there yesterday; surely they must have a vision of something? I remember seeing the one in the tree that took the brunt of the collision, so cutting down that specific tree may have been a deliberate action too.'

Soop responded. 'We think so too, but can't get access to the vision without a subpoena. That doesn't happen unless we have decided to treat the accident as a fraud attempt.' Rose nodded. 'Oh, that makes sense. Otherwise, everybody would want to see their five minutes of fame on the small screen.'

Nic smiled. 'I can access them, but I'll have to make a phone call. Let's see where the evidence takes us. We'll have another card up our sleeve when we have the footage.'

They found only a couple of photos with the vision of the cameras and were reviewing more pictures when there was a knock at the door. It was the Ambulance Officer. 'Oh, good, you're all still here. You might want to see this.'

She went over to the iPad and pulled up a Facebook link: *'Looking for a place to crash tonight?'* They watched the vision. 'Wait for it……there.'

The Lead Investigator stopped the vision. It was a picture of the Britannia Roundabout, taken around 4 p.m. Thursday, and showed a van parked next to one of the camera poles. A ladder was fully extended against the pole, and a young man was halfway up.

'It's against their safety protocols to be up a ladder without a spotter, but it may not mean anything. I was sent the vision by one of my tech guys. We are required to review everything when an accident occurs at the roundabout. A lobby group is still trying to change it to traffic lights, even after all these years.'

Nic nodded. 'OK, but how did you get this?'

'It's all part of an agreement between the South Australian Ambulance Service and the Government. We get the vision eight hours prior and eight hours after any accident that's more than a scraping of paint.'

The two Investigators 'high-fived,' then they looked towards Rose and Nic for confirmation, but Rose returned to her notebook. 'Sorry guys, it doesn't make sense. You said the accident happened around three in the morning, so if this vision is time-stamped at four, it's outside that time window. It's more than eight hours.' They looked at her, then at the Ambulance Officer. 'OK, then I'll need to check that out to ensure the date and time stamp are correct.'

Nic interrupted. 'I'll get my computer guy to look at it too. We don't know how big this Insurance scam is so someone could be inside the Traffic Control Systems, or the vision might have been doctored.'

Soop nodded. 'But you won't be able to access it without a subpoena either.'

Nic smiled. 'It's OK. I'll make another phone call. Will do. What else have you got in your little black book, Rose? Anything about me...?'

'Nope, there are not enough pages.'

The Ambulance Officer then saluted. 'I'll leave this to you guys to sort out then. I'll be in touch. Jay, congrats on your recent wedding, too. You might have to reconsider the double-barrelled surname; sometimes it doesn't quite work.' Soop laughed and shook her hand as she departed the room.

'As soon as we know, you'll know.'

'I know.'

Rose prompted him about the name. 'So what's your surname then?'

''Kent-Clarke'. I was Jay Kent, and I married Jasmine Clarke.'

Rose smiled. 'It's no wonder they call you 'Soop'. Did you work for the 'Daily Planet' in a previous life? Or tend to avoid kryptonite?'

Nic finally caught up. 'So, reverse the names, and it becomes 'Clark-Kent'. Rose's mother has a similar issue, as she calls herself Jana Wilkinson. Her married name is Palmer, so she is Palmer-Jana.'

Another person had joined them in the room, but they hadn't noticed during all the light-hearted banter. It was the South Australian Commissioner of Police, Gerard Steldons. Nic turned, smiled, and they shook hands. 'Enough with the funny stuff, Mr Thorn; this is serious.'

'Good to see you again, Gerry. Do you remember Rose? And this is Jay 'Soop' Kent-Clarke and Penn Brophy from the Accident Investigations Team.'

'Good to see Rose is still with you. I've met Soop and Penn before.'

'So what brings you to the Hospital, Gerry?'

'I was here doing a catch-up with the 'Heads Of', so I thought I'd walk through the corridors. I always make a point of going through the Emergency Ward to see what my guys have been up to overnight and what happened whilst I was sleeping. I met the doctor who had treated the patients from your accident, and he told me his private thoughts.'

'Ok, so does he think it's an accident scam?'

'Sorry Nic, F.M.E.O.'

Rose nodded. 'In this case ', ears only', not 'eyes' Nic.'

'Yep, I got that part, Rose. Gee, you're catching on quickly to all this investigation stuff.'

'Well, it's been over three years, and we have looked into about fifteen scams together.'

'But doesn't time fly when you're having fun?' They all looked at Gerry. 'Well, I wouldn't call what I do as fun, looking into the belly of the beast. I'll leave you guys to sort out this latest thing; please let me know if you need a hand with anything.' He then left the room.

Soop looked at Penn. 'Wow, he remembered us. I didn't think what we do went further up the line.'

Nic nodded. 'You two guys have a great reputation for solving stuff, helping out with stuff, and giving a stuff. It is noticed. '

Soop nodded. 'Thanks, Nic. Anyway, do you want to come with us to do the interviews? I've just got a text to let me know the driver and passenger are both conscious and ready to talk.'

Nic nodded. 'Yep, let's do it, but it would be best if Rose and I stay out of the process. I'll organise a couple of disguises so we can observe.'

Rose shook her head. 'Damn you, Nic.'

Nic grinned. 'Rose, I'll be delivering food into the ward, and you can wear a white coat, and hang a stethoscope around your neck to look like a Doctor.'

'Yep, that will work.'

CHAPTER 8

They set up the interview in the ward and Soop and Penn made their way to the driver. They were advised that although he was barely conscious, he was willing to give an initial interview. Rose entered the space next to the patient and pulled the curtain behind her, then nodded to Nic, who was slowly shuffling around dealing with the meal trays.

The interview began, and Soop took the lead: 'Good afternoon, and thanks for seeing us so quickly after your accident. The Doctor has said that the injuries are not life-threatening. However, there may be long-term effects. It may include not being able to drive a car again.' He waited for a reaction from the patient, but there was none, then continued. 'We are here today to get an understanding of what happened, and we apologise for the interview being so close to the event, but the longer we leave it, the memory changes things. Are you OK to proceed?'

The young man nodded slowly.

'Firstly, sorry for your loss.'

They watched as the man's pupils dilated; the statement had been made to prompt a reaction.

'Err. What loss? Who died?' The reaction was quick and strong.

Soop continued: 'Oops, I meant the loss of your car. It's a write-off, but we'll deal with that part later. We're more worried about how the accident occurred. Can you tell us what happened?'

The young man nodded his head and settled back down into the bed. 'I'd just left a friend's party. I hadn't been drinking or doing drugs. There were three of us in the car. I was driving well under the speed limit. It was dark. I think about three o'clock. I was turning left towards the city and was going to get a burger from the place on the end of Hindley Street, in West Terrace.' The man began to cough. 'Water, can I have water, please.'

Soop handed him the plastic tumbler, and the man slowly sipped it. 'Can you continue?'

He nodded. 'The roundabout. I slowed down, but a car came from my right. I went to stomp on the brake, but I hit the accelerator instead. I think I hit the other car. I crashed into the middle, where all the bushes were. I hit the tree and blacked out. I can't remember much else.'

'OK, thank you. How fast do you think you were going when you hit the tree?'

'Well.' He gulped and took a breath. 'I would say about fifty, maybe fifty-five.'

Soop nodded. 'Do you know what happened to your passenger?'

'I think he's in here somewhere too. Did you find the other car? He'll confirm what happened.'

'Did you know the other driver? How do you know it was a he?'

'Um....I don't ...I think I must rest now if that's OK.' The young man closed his eyes and turned his head away. Penn nodded, then looked over to Soop.

'We'll leave it for now, but we appreciate your time today. Thank you.'

They moved away and headed for the other patient, but Nic stayed in the room, set his phone on a meal tray, and pushed the record on the camera app. The patient didn't stir, so Nic then dropped a tray onto the ground and watched as his patient reacted. The young man shot up suddenly, looked over to Nic, gave him a 'one finger' salute, and then settled back into the bed with a grin.

Rose came quickly out from her shrouded area, glared at Nic, and rushed to him. 'What was that for?'

'A simple test, Rose. He failed.' Nic then exited the room, followed quickly by Rose, and they made their way down the corridor to meet with the others.

The interview with the second patient was less forthcoming. However, Soop pressed the matters anyway: 'I'm sorry to do this, but we've just interviewed your friend and need to check some details before we pass the information onto the compensation people. It's a quick process if you need access to some money to cover these medical expenses.'

The young man shook his head, his voice husky, but managed a response: 'This is a Public Hospital. There are no other expenses if you are brought in by Ambulance after a car crash.'

Penn shook her head. 'I'm sorry, but that's not the case. There's the cost of the Ambulance, and yes, whilst the driver is covered, passengers are not. And in your case, you look like you need a skin graft on that nasty burn on your hand. It may not be covered at all.'

The young man looked at Soop, then over to Penn. 'I'm not feeling that good. Can you please leave?'

'Yes, we will very soon, but you might have to speed up your recovery process; the longer you stay here, the more it will cost you. They'll assess your injuries and decide how long you can stay before sending you to a Private Ward. That's when costs start to mount up. We're sorry, it might get expensive for you.'

'OK, I get it.'

'Can we ask one more question, though?'

'OK, if you must.'

'The driver said he was going through the roundabout and heading for the twenty-four-hour Bakery on Norwood Parade. I love that place; what's your go-to pastry? They do a great pie-floater there too.'

'I don't know....um, a Custard Slice. I've never had a floater, however. Is that the meat pie they serve in a bowl of mushy peas?'

'Yes, it's an Adelaide delicacy. What about the other bloke in the back seat? What do you reckon his favourite is? I'm sure you were talking about it.'

'Yeah, yeah. She was going to have the Cornish pasty. She's over from the...um...the Yorke Peninsula and can't get enough of them. I need to rest now. Can you leave, please?'

Soop and Penn finalised their notes and left the room. 'Thank you for your time, and I hope you're feeling better soon.'

Nic and Rose followed them out, and they all returned to the office to collate the findings. Once they had sat down, Soop started first. 'What a crock. Their stories aren't even the same, and the first guy didn't mention 'Isabella,' whilst the second guy referred to a 'she's over from the YP' wanting to find a Cornish pasty at three o'clock in the morning.'

Rose piped up. 'And there's more. The driver said he was turning left towards the city, but you don't enter the roundabout to do that, there's a slip road. He also said 'I' a lot, meaning he was likely to be the only one in the car.'

Soop nodded. 'Yes, it's so sad that the young guys think it's OK to scam insurance companies, but unless we can get a confession or enough to proceed with a fraud case, it will be dismissed as a car accident. He'll lose his new car, and that's about it.'

'The Supra?'

'Yes, we can go after that too. If we can prove anything fictitious on the loan application, we can apply to re-possess the car.'

Rose looked at her notes. 'Did he get it through a Finance Company?'

'Yes, and that's why their car loans are cheaper, as they take the car as security, and the major Banks tend not to do this.'

Rose nodded. 'They don't think it through do they?'

Soop smiled. 'Yes, and he's smashed his mother's car. It's registered to her, so she gets nothing either.'

Nic stood up. 'Where to from here then, Soop?'

Soop took a moment to refer to his notes. 'Gather more evidence, work out how and why the traffic cameras were not operating, get the car removed and taken to our warehouse for a closer review, work out if the grass fire has anything to do with it, and then get the Police involved. Oh, and work out who or where Isabella Swan is and how she managed to get released from the hospital without being formally interviewed.'

'So, not much more?'

Soop looked at him, and Nic continued. 'Hey, I've got four other guys ready to help. Seiko is a Policewoman, having a couple of days R and R here in Adelaide, and can put her police spin on it but can't make the arrest. Do you have anyone that you use?'

'Not really, we usually have lots of hoops to jump through.'

'I can make a call and change that if you like. Gerry Steldons will give you a name to whom you can refer these cases if the evidence stacks up. If not, they'll work with you to ensure it can.'

Penn looked at him. 'Really?'

Rose looked at them. 'Absolutely, guys. We all have to work together with this scamming stuff.'

Nic nodded. 'What she said. Hang on, Rose, have you got anything else?'

Rose referred to her notes. 'Sort of. The driver said he was 'well under' the speed limit but hit 'fifty or fifty-five' when his foot slipped onto the accelerator. The road width at the roundabout is only two lanes, so he's somehow jumped warp speed in a fifteen-year-old Holden and launched upwards into a tree.'

Penn looked at her. 'Anything else?'

'Oh, and I reviewed the photos from the accident. There is damage on the left-hand passenger door panel, and as he said, the car was coming from the right, so how can there be damage on the left?'

'And anything more?'

'Well, it's a bit of a leap, but I've been thinking about the grass fire and the ring burn on the passenger's palm. I noticed a necklace on the small grey chest of drawers next to the bed. It had a three three-pointed symbol hanging from the end. A circle and the letter Y looked like a Mercedes Benz emblem. Can I borrow your iPad for a minute?'

Soop nodded and handed it over. Rose then made a few keystrokes and pulled up a view from the movie 1981 'Indiana Jones and the Raider of the Lost Ark'; it showed one of the German villains with a wound etched into the palm of his hand and spun the tablet around for the others to see. 'This guy probably picked up the metal ring emblem from a fire.' Rose looked at the photo, then over to Nic.

'So, is there something else you need to tell us?'

'Err... they could've been the same kids from the airport that damaged our van and most likely lit the fire at the roundabout to destroy evidence. He may have accidentally dropped the emblem into it, then tried to retrieve it, and it burnt into his hand?'

'Yep, that will do.'

Soop nodded. 'So can we add another crime to them? The wilful destruction of property? And arson?'

'There's no actual evidence these guys did it. So, unless they confess, it will just be an insurance claim. Do you know of any good Insurance Investigators?'

They both laughed and Nic continued: 'There's nothing else to do now; these two scammers aren't going anywhere, so let's call it a day and head back to the Hotel.'

Soop nodded. 'Sure, and thanks for everything, guys. We'll wind this up tomorrow and bring in the Police to manage the rest of the case once we've finalised the investigation.'

Rose piped up. 'Sorry, but I have some more stuff. It turns out that Sandy's father is part of the 'Circle of Community Change'. They are citizens lobbying to get rid of the roundabouts all over Adelaide. His group sits at the roundabouts and takes down details of the number of crashes, so I'm sure there will be someone that recorded the details of the man with the van doing what he can to take out the span of the cameras.'

Nic nodded, called an Uber, and they said their goodbyes.

When they arrived back at the Atura Hotel, they met with Sandy at the Hangar Bar. The three others arrived about half an hour later and sat with them to review the case's developments. It was decided that Dee-Dee and Seiko could return to Brisbane and start looking into the scratch-and-win investigation. Sandy, Rose, and Nic would remain in Adelaide to assist in finalising the case against the motor vehicle accident scammers.

Nic looked at Rose and Sandy. 'You know that we have the morning free, you can go to the Burnside Shopping Village to buy the outfits for our lunch meeting with the Department of Housing on Friday.'

Rose responded. 'We've already ordered a UBER to take us to the Airport DFO. They do have late-night shopping here in Adelaide.'

Nic, Rose, and Sandy made it to the Housing Trust luncheon but 'The She Shed" didn't win the contract.

CHAPTER 9

In the morning, Driver collected Nic, Sandy, and Rose, and they headed back to meet with Sandy's father at the Britannia Hotel for another look around. Nic had met Robb Fraser previously. They entered the restaurant.

'Good to see you again, Robb. It's a bit early for a whiskey, but I've got a bottle of something I thought we might like to try later.' Nic handed over a bottle of Laphroaig, a 25-year-old Malt Whiskey.

Robb smiled, then dropped his backpack onto the table, opened it, and withdrew a gift bag. He, too, had brought along a bottle to give to Nic. It was of the same brand. 'Good choice, Mr Thorn, but why?'

'For keeping a watchful eye on things.'

Robb nodded, and then Nic nodded, too. 'And the bottle for me?'

'Same thing.' Rose and Sandy smiled.

Robb leaned forward in his chair. 'Anyway, enough of this emotional stuff. I heard you want to look at the diaries of this roundabout that our Citizens Circle keeps. Anything in particular, or do you want to join our lobby group?'

'Nope, but thanks for the offer. We want to know if anyone was around the place last Thursday at about four p.m. as the traffic cameras may have been re-directed or disabled.'

Robb pulled his Tablet from the backpack, logged in, and swiped to a spreadsheet. 'Ok, that was Bill.' He then turned the screen around to show Nic, and the rows across the top of the screen read 'Bill, Bill, Bill, Bill, and Bill.'

Sandy looked at it. 'That's a lot of Bills. I thought you sat there too?'

'Yes, I'm the third Bill. It's all about maintaining anonymity. We change the locations and use the same names.' He pointed to a second column with two alphabet letters. 'Each letter is the place; in this case, 'BK' is the Britannia Roundabout, as in 'Britannia - Kensington.''

Sandy looked at him. 'There's a roundabout at Blackwood. Do you use a 'B' for that too?'

'Nope. We use 'VBC'– as in 'Very-B-Cold.'' He then explained that each time the volunteers finished their shift, an email was sent to their website detailing anything significant. Robb swiped back to the date and opened the sub-folder. It was entitled 'Anything of Significance', and another folder was titled 'Weird Stuff'. He reviewed the first folder and declared nothing noteworthy from four crashes and three near misses in a four-hour shift.

The waiter came over, took a drinks order, and checked if anyone was having breakfast. They ordered coffee and a chai latte for Nic.

Sandy looked at the spreadsheet. 'So, Dad, how long have you been doing this 'Circle' thing? It looks like sitting around doing nothing when you could be doing something.'

'It's not that bad and gives us blokes something else to talk about instead of our health, and besides, most of the wives refuse to be involved, they reckon it's too boring. It's like a 'Men's Shed' but watching cars, instead of watching each other building wooden cars.'

'How much time do you spend alone then?'

'We're not alone. We all have these Tablet things and can hook into a free Wi-Fi signal if it's strong enough. We also read books and drink lots of coffee. We've tried fishing, golf, and playing cards and reckon we're too young for lawn bowls, so we watch the cars go around roundabouts and record things.'

'So, did you find anything?'

'Yes, Bill does a good job with 'Weird Stuff'. He's made a note about a guy adjusting the traffic cameras. Generally, we talk to the technicians, but in this case, he's written. 'FMO'.'

Rose looked at him. 'Found Me Out?'

Robb shook his head, so Sandy tried to guess. 'Free Make Over?'

Driver had a go. 'Free Mandarins and Oranges?'

Nic smiled. 'I assume it means 'Fobbed Me Off.'

'You're correct, Nic. Give the man a bottle of whiskey for guessing correctly. Hang on, I already did.'

Sandy looked at him. 'What else did Bill note down.'

'Well, he took a long, long, hard look at the guy's driver's license and took down the details of the van registration plate. That's probably against the law. Over to you, Nic.'

Nic nodded. 'It could be classified as a form of stalking, but in the interest of the bigger picture, I think we could forgive Bill, but how did he get the Drivers Licence?'

'He sort of took his wallet from the van when the dude was up the ladder.'

'Err, that's definitely against the law. Does he still have it?'

'Probably. Why?'

'We can use it as our 'in' to snoop and see what's what. I'll arrange to give it back to him. Can we meet with Bill now?'

'Sure. He'll probably be at St Theodore's Church in Rose Park, where he's a lay preacher. We can walk there if you like.'

The group walked southwards along Fullarton Road, left into Grant Avenue, and stood outside the Anglican Church. Robb went inside, located 'Bill', and they were welcomed.

Sandy looked at her Father, then looked at the Father. 'I'm sorry, Father; I must confess it's been a while since I've been to Church.'

Sandy held her hand out and lightly gathered the priest's hand. 'No worries, Love, but we don't do confessional here, we're Anglicans.'

Robb nodded. 'So Bill, they are looking into the smash early Thursday morning, and the note you posted about that guy up the ladder might be relevant to the investigation. Have you still got his wallet?'

The priest lowered his head. 'I'm sorry. I did indeed steal his wallet and must confess I have not yet returned it. I also removed the cash and donated to the Church. I left a receipt in case he wants to claim a tax deduction.' He removed the wallet from under his cassock and handed it to Robb.

The group returned to the Britannia Hotel for an early lunch. Meals were served, and Nic located the property on his map app. 'I hate to say this, guys, but this bloke lives in Modbury, and it's about a twenty-minute drive.'

The group said farewells to Robb, drove north-eastwards via Lower North East Road, and pulled into the Tea Tree Plaza Shopping Centre car park. They stopped there to decide their next move.

Driver looked over to Nic. 'So how do we run this? Hello Sir, I believe this is your wallet?'

Nic went to step out of the car. 'Nope, I'll tell him the truth. A priest found it and asked me to deliver it back to you. I'll do this on my own.'

Sandy nodded. 'OK, but what do you want us to do? Stay in the car with the window down a little and a bowl of water?'

'well. You still have a Credit Card, and we're outside one of Adelaide's largest suburban shopping centres. I'm sure Driver would love to show you around.'

Rose nodded. 'Well, it's not exactly the Burnside Shops, but there is a new restaurant over the other side linked to the chain that we are investigating as part of the scratch-and-win scam. We could check that out.'

'OK, but just don't win anything.'

Rose continued: 'How long will you need?'

'I don't know. It looks like about a ten-minute walk to the house. I'll have a look around and meet you at the restaurant in about half an hour. If I'm not back in forty, come looking for me.'

They separated, and Driver turned to Rose and Sandy once Nic had moved out of sight. 'I'm going to follow him, guys; I hope that's OK. My Spidey senses tell me to be careful; he might need backup.'

'Wow, we thought your superpower was being invisible. We never saw you at the Car Show inside the Convention Centre the first time you worked with us here in Adelaide.' Driver nodded. 'I have inter-changeable superpowers. You should see what I can do when I get stopped for speeding. My Mind Control ability is out of this world.'

'So you've had success avoiding the fines?'

'Not entirely, but I've never been caught speeding, so something must be working.'

Rose and Sandy hugged him and waited to see where Driver was going. Then, I saw him collide with an empty shopping trolley, which started rolling towards a group of parked cars. He ran after it and managed to tip it over before it had done any damage, but the metallic crash resounded loudly through the car park.

Rose looked at Sandy. 'So much for being invisible. I guess some superpowers can wear off. Who knew?'

Meantime, Nic was wandering down Reservoir Road, made a left-hand turn into the second street and expected the house to be at the end of the cul-de-sac. There was a Cable Van parked outside the house. Nic made his way to the front door and pressed the doorbell. There was no response, so he knocked. Nic was also getting a sense that he was being watched. 'Hello, hello, is anybody home.'

Nic stepped back from the door when he heard a very loud 'woof', but no one came to the door, so he decided to inspect the Cable Van and was considering his next option when a deep voice came from inside the house: 'Go away. I'm not buying anything.'

A man had come to the door and was holding the leash of a large black bullmastiff. The dog was huge, but fortunately, the man had it under control, at least from behind the security door. Nic called out. 'I've got a wallet. I think it could be yours. I work in the hospital. My priest found it.'

The reply came: 'Hold it up.'

Nic obeyed the direction and held it up.

'Did you take the money from inside it?'

'Nope, there's about one hundred and twenty in there.' Nic realised that the 'donation exchange' wasn't a good idea, and had replaced the cash with his own.

'OK, come forward. What were you doing at my van?'

'Nothing. I wondered if I should leave the wallet on the windshield or try to slip it inside.'

'You just can't trust anyone around here. OK, come to the door. I'll let you in, and you can tell me exactly how you found it. When I saw it last, I was working on the cameras at the Kensi roundabout. It was on the seat, and when I returned, it was gone. You reckon your priest found it then?'

The man let him inside, and Nic carefully made his way around the dog, but there wasn't much room. Nic handed over the wallet, and the man slowly counted the cash. 'It's still got the one hundred and twenty dollars. Tell me about this priest?'

'Sure, but can I please have a glass of water? It's a little warm out there today, and the walk from the hospital took longer than I thought.'

The man looked at him suspiciously and told the dog to sit, which it did, and he left the room. Nic then carefully stood up, maneuvered around the dog, and went around the room looking for things of interest, but the only item he found was a blank invoice from the Traffic Control Centre in Norwood. He took a picture with his camera but wasn't quick enough to sit back down.

'What did you just do?'

'Nothing. I stood up and stretched. The back of my shirt is sweaty from the walk.'

The man looked at him. 'Uh-huh,' then he approached a tiny blue box on the fireplace's mantle. He hooked a cable into his phone and viewed the vision. 'So, what's so important about that invoice then?'

Nic recognised the box as an Atom Stream Cop Camera as he'd used them himself. 'Err. I was wondering where that Traffic Control Centre was. I didn't realise it was at Norwood.'

'Uh-huh. I think you should go now. I didn't catch your name. Why is that Mr Mysterious?'

Nic started to walk back towards the front door, keeping one eye on the big dog and the other on the man. 'OK, OK, I'm leaving. I dropped your wallet back. It's the honest truth.'

'Uh-huh, but next time you replace cash, find out what denomination it was. It was one hundred and twenty dollars, but it was six twenty dollar notes, not two fifties and two tens. Hercules likes to bite those pesky door-to-door salesmen, so I'm sure he'll enjoy nipping at your heels, too.'

Nic quickly returned to the door, which had already been opened before he arrived and looked up to see that Driver had opened it. Nic burst through the door.

'Big dog. Driver, run.'

Nic ran out the door and passed the van before he realised that Driver wasn't behind him; then he heard Driver call out. 'Hey, you, dog. Run this way, you big boofy, box-headed.....' Driver took off in the opposite direction, and the big, dopey, box-headed dog loped after him.

Nic had stopped running and watched Driver doing his best to keep in front of the pursuit, dodging and weaving the best that a one-hundred-and-thirty-kilogram man could, running in Blundstone Work boots. Suddenly Driver changed direction and ran down the side of a house. Nic heard a gate slam shut and then the dog barking loudly. A few minutes later, Driver came around from the other side of the house with a big grin.

'I don't think there's anyone home, but the dog's owner won't be happy as it's stuck inside someone else's backyard.' Nic smiled, and they started walking back to the shopping centre.

On the way, Nic called and put on a frightened young girl's voice the best he could: 'Hello, is that the Council Dog Patrol? There's a big black dog in my backyard, and it's very angry....'

Meantime, Sandy and Rose were sitting in the restaurant anxiously waiting for Nic and Driver to return. They'd drunk their third glass of water, and the waitress was getting antsy with them as they wouldn't order anything else.

Finally, the men arrived and sat down.

'We have to order something or leave, Nic.'

Driver nodded. 'Have you checked out the menu? I'm in the mood for a big hot dog.'

CHAPTER 10

As they were driving back into the city Nic decided to check out the middle of the roundabout again, but when they arrived, they noticed that the Holden Camira had been removed. He called Soop. 'Hi Soop, did you manage to get the car removed? ....OK, yes, we can do that. See you in about an hour then.' Nic disconnected and then addressed his group.

'OK, guys, we can go back to the centre of the roundabout and check out the foliage or go straight to the recovery warehouse to watch them go over the car. What do you want to do?'

Rose looked up from her notes. 'Let's go to the roundabout. We know the direction of the cameras had been tampered with, but why wouldn't the Traffic Control Centre have noticed and sent someone to investigate?'

Nic responded after some thought. 'It was after four p.m., so maybe the work jobs aren't allocated until the next day?'

'Nope, I checked that too. The two teams work a six-hour shift, from six in the morning to six at night.'

'How did you find that out?'

'I have a go-to computer guy.'

Nic nodded. 'What's his name? Do I know him?'

'It's Chiwetel Bacher.'

'Nope, I don't know him. I hope he's good and won't mind playing second fiddle to my Chewy.'

'Oh no, he's as good a Chewy. You could say they're a mirror image of each other.'

'Why?'

'You didn't know that is Chewy's real name?'

'Duh, of course, it is, but I haven't heard that name for about thirty years. How did you get it out of him?'

'I asked him what it was like being named after a big brown Wookie thing from one of those Star thingy movies. He laughed and told me it wasn't his real name, so he told me, just like that.'

'You know what that means now, don't you?'

'Nope.'

'He'll have to change his name. Please don't ask Driver what *his* real name is.'

'Can we have a guess?'

Driver piped up. 'Nope, it's a secret, but I will tell you I'm named after a famous writer.'

'Wow, your real name is R.R Tolkien or maybe J.K Rowling?'

He laughed. 'No, a little bit earlier.'

Rose responded. 'Ok then, how about Murasaki Shikibu?'

'Who's that?'

'Reported to be the writer of the world's first novel, published in Japan around a thousand years ago. I once got that question in a University Game Show.'

Nic shook his head. 'Enough. Next, you'll be asking me what my real name is.'

'Oh, we know that already. It's Nigel No-friends.'

'Wow, that's nasty. I have friends; it's just that they all seem to be busy when I call.'

'You started it. When we met, I told you I never wanted to be a Rose Thorn, yet you continue giving us silly names.'

'Duly noted, 'Rose To-The-Occasion.' We're here, so let's get this investigation underway.'

Driver stopped the car at the back of the Britannia Hotel, and they made their way across the traffic to the centre of the roundabout. They located the charred ground and burnt grass but noticed that the site had been cleared when the car had been collected. Even the tree with the fork that Rose had photographed had been entirely removed. 'This isn't good, Nic.'

'Nope. Soop didn't mention that the site had been cleared. It's all a little odd. Anyway, there's nothing more we can do here, and it looks like the cameras have been re-aligned too. After looking at the car, we might need to visit the Traffic Control Centre at Norwood.'

Rose nodded. 'How about we look at where all the cameras are located from the photos taken the other day, and how many needed to be re-directed?'

'Good idea, I'll go first. I spy with my little eye, something that starts with a 'c'.'

'Car.' Driver blurted out quickly.

'Callistemon', Sandy called out, then added. 'They are the only bushes left in the middle that weren't removed. Maybe they ran out of time or were interrupted.'

'Clue.' Rose noted quietly, then walked over to the Callistemon hedge and pointed out the remnants of a red bicycle helmet. It was still mostly intact, including the inner foam shell. However, it was partially melted and blackened with soot. 'I guess whoever tidied up didn't see the red helmet amongst the red flowers.'

Nic took a picture of it amongst the bushes, then sent it by SMS to Soop and paused for a moment before ringing him. 'Hey Soop, we're at the roundabout again. Did you get the picture of the helmet I just sent you?'

Driver went to pick it out of the bush, but Rose held up her hand to tell him to wait for Nic to disconnect the call. Nic gave a 'thumbs up'.

'It's OK, Driver, we have permission to collect it as evidence. People who do these types of accident scams often wear helmets. Well spotted, Rose.'

Rose reached into her backpack and extracted a small pair of tongs and a plastic bag, collected the helmet, dropped it in, sealed it, and handed it to Nic with an adhesive sticker and a pen so he could initial and date it.

'Wow, you're getting good at this secret search, seize, and spy stuff.'

Rose nodded. 'Yes, Nic. I'm still learning from the best of the rest on the internet. Did you know over seventy actors have played Sherlock Holmes?'

Nic nodded. 'I do now, and I especially liked the one played by Iron Man. Anyway, let's move on to where the car was taken and review the rest of the evidence. To the airport, Driver and don't spare the horsepower.'

They left the roundabout and went through the outskirts of the Central Business District, then along Sir Donald Bradman Drive via the suburb of Hilton. Sandy pointed out the Hilton Hotel, at Hilton, not to be confused with the Hilton Hotel in the Central Business District.

Rose nodded. 'Thanks, Sandy, but I'm still wondering why they named them both The Hilton Hotel.'

Driver piped up. 'Which one?'

'Both of them. There are so many better names you can make up these days.'

Driver nodded. 'It's just another conundrum we South Australians have to face, along with how we lost the Australian Grand Prix to Victoria in 1995.'

They arrived at the airport turnoff, Driver then took a left at the first street and stopped by the warehouse where Soop and Penn were waiting. Soop took possession of the evidence. 'Good pickup with the helmet, Rose.' He hefted it for weight and rolled it over. 'I would say it's too small for a man so that it could belong to the elusive Isabella Swan.' He directed the group through the hangar door and showed them to the Holden. It was now up on a hoist.

'You were correct, Rose. There's not enough damage to the car's underside to indicate a collision. I suspect they chose a quiet moment to drive in there and then winched it into place.'

Rose nodded. 'That would take some organisation too. They'd need a truck or a small crane on the back of a Ute.'

Soop and Penn then moved them into an office where they had set up whiteboards and a table was littered with documentary evidence. The boards showed timelines starting from 4 p.m. and included pictures of the 'Cable Van' along with the name and address of the alleged driver of the Holden. There was also a picture of a young woman. She looked about eighteen and was dressed in an outfit for a formal, most likely from a high school graduation. There was a picture of another car, a Dodge RAM utility, with a small crane in the rear tray.

Nic collected the helmet and walked over to the photo of the young woman. 'Where did you get this picture, Soop? This could belong to her.'

Rose looked it over. 'Did you check inside the helmet? Perhaps there's a name?' Nic handed the evidence bag to Penn, and she broke the seal. 'You know, you didn't need to seal it as we don't have any Police protocols to follow. We don't have access to DNA testing either.'

'Yep, but Rose did a good job, surely we can't be that lucky with the helmet?'

Penn opened the bag carefully, lifted out the helmet, and took a closer look. 'Don't you just love people and their need to label their possessions?' There was a label underneath a foam strip:

'If found, please call 015572672.'

Penn continued. 'Well, we found more about their little posse on Facebook. The young woman is the friend of the utility driver. Her name is Amity Reilly. She's at University studying veterinary science, and there's a Facebook link back to her. He's a Dental Surgeon at the Royal Adelaide Hospital, so we could assume she might have access to the propofol and know how to administer injections.'

Rose pondered the situation. 'That's a dangerous way to earn a couple of bucks.'

Penn nodded and continued. 'Anyway, we haven't interviewed her yet. We made a call to her father only to get the standard response: "You're not going to interview my child without the presence of my lawyer."'

Nic nodded this time. 'Shall we make a phone call to find out who owns the helmet?' Soop took the direction, cleared his throat, and started practising a narrative with a young man's voice. He held his finger to his mouth to tell the others to be quiet, rang the number, and a young woman quickly answered it.

'Hello, this is Amity. Who's this?'

'Hi, my name is Chill. I found your helmet. It was in the bushes at the Kensi roundabout. I was hurrying through it, and like some doofus, cut me off. I smashed into the bush and like broke my board.'

'Bummer. Like when was this?'

'About six, early morning Thurs. I was like heading to work at Macca's.'

'Is the helmet all busted up?'

'Nup. It's all good. Do ya want it back? Where 'bouts are you?'

'I'll send you my address. Can you drop it off now? I really need it.'

The address came through via SMS to his phone: 'Great, got it. Like give me an hour, and I'll be there.'

Soop disconnected. 'I do hope her father's home, as I'd love to see how he stops us from talking to her this time.'

Driver looked at him. 'So, your car or ours?'

Penn responded. 'Nope, it will be a call from the Police for that. We can only make the enquiries and don't have to go that far into it. Although, we will have the two guys in the hospital charged with Insurance fraud, arson, or just being a waste of time. We're not quite sure yet, as there's no actual crime for being stupid.' Rose responded. 'So, what about the guy in the Ute? Did you catch up with him? And did you get anywhere with an investigation at the Traffic Control Centre?'

'Yes, to most of that. It's all in the brief that we are presenting to our newly allocated Police Liaison Officer, thanks to a call from the Police Commissioner.'

Nic smiled, and Penn nodded, then walked to the evidence table and picked up an evidence folder. 'I had a nice chat with the TCC General Manager earlier today. It turns out a couple of his staff have suddenly taken leave.' Penn then pulled out a headshot of a man in his late forties.

'This guy, Lincoln Driver, looked after the cameras and site maintenance. He's also suspected of the involvement in the premature clearing of the middle of the roundabout earlier today and was rostered on when the cameras were re-directed.' Penn tapped at the photo of the utility with a small crane in the rear.

'And this is his truck.'

Soop then took over. 'And this young man, Kaleb Driver, who calls himself 'Kab', turns out to be the nephew of Lincoln. They had a nice little scam going, and it looks like we've got another couple of 'accidents' to look into, spanning over the last eighteen months or so.' He then held up a photo of a Nissan 300Z. 'And this is *his* car.'

Nic moved in to take a closer look. 'So, they're AWOL, I assume?'

'Yes, Lincoln is heading west, and Kab north, into the Northern Territory. They have about four hours on us.' He looked over to Nic. 'Your little home visit, under the guise of the return of wallet thing, must have spooked them into evasive action as we immediately picked up some chatter on Messenger. We have the local State Police involved, so we expect them to be stopped at the state borders. If they get that far.'

Sandy grinned. 'You said they are Lincoln Driver and Kab Driver?' She looked over at Driver. 'So are they relatives of yours then?'

'I don't think so. I only have one name.'

Penn and Soop started assembling the evidence and removing the photos from the boards. 'Another win for the good guys, and thanks, Nic and your team, for all your help.'

Nic nodded. 'Well, at least there is some good news. It's a short walk back to the Hotel Atura from here. I love it when a plan comes together.'

Rose looked at him. 'We didn't do anything apart from turning up. How do you justify your expense if that's all we do?'

'Well, if we can help bring down another scammer without hurting anyone, surely that's a good thing?'

'Ok, I'll give you that. 'Nic Thorn and Associates, we do little or do a lot. It doesn't matter if no one gets shot and scammers lose the plot.'

'Well, there is that, Rose.'

CHAPTER 11

A week later, Nic, Rose and Dee-Dee were on the rear deck in West End, Brisbane, having an early dinner. Sandy had remained in Adelaide to spend time with her Father, and Seiko was absent doing actual police work. Dog was sitting on Nic's lap, and the little 'Teacup' Pekinese dog, Goliath, from next door was sitting on the top step, watching for any unwanted intruders.

The pizzas were delivered, and they all spent time keeping Dog from claiming the prawn toppings. Goliath, of course, remained focused on his mission. Dee-Dee stood up and poured another round of drinks. 'I heard the Adelaide thing wound up pretty quickly in the end?'

'Yep, once they brought everyone together and sat them in the same room, they started turning on each other. It turned out that when the police got hold of Amity's phone, it revealed the group's activities. You have to love kids and their desire to keep everyone informed. They had a 'What's App' site linking everyone in and used 'Meeting Place' for the gatherings, so it just came down to getting a subpoena in order.'

'Wow, I thought that only happens in the movies.'

'Add a little bit of heat, then a little bit of cold. There was no food or water, and with Kenny G. Muzak on an endless loop through the sound speakers, it would turn anyone. Amity knew we couldn't access the phone records without her password, but if you have the right connections with the phoney people at Apple, they will let you have a peek if you don't leave a trace. Chewy is one person who knows those people.'

Dee-Dee brushed Dog's paw away. 'Have you got something to feed the cat, please?'

Rose nodded and opened a smaller pizza box. 'Sure, we've ordered him his pizza.' Nic took a slice, picked off a prawn, fed it to Dog, then leaned down to his suitcase and produced the brief regarding the 'scratch and win' cards.

'Are you ready for the next investigation?'

They all nodded, and Dog hiccupped, then he stopped eating for a moment to check if anyone noticed. Nic continued: 'Well, their investigation had not revealed anything more, but we have confirmed the winning ticket prizes are only being distributed in Australia, so it looks like we're not going offshore with this one. The restaurant chain has stores in all capital cities and some country locations. We might be spread a little thin on the ground until we can pinpoint the source and identity of the perpetrators.'

Dee-Dee nodded and reviewed the list. 'Every location? I've just Googled them, and there are over ninety stores in Australia. So what are the prizes? I haven't seen anything on Facebook, Instagram, or even local papers getting in on the act. I would've thought the whole idea was about a marketing opportunity, so they're missing out.'

Nic nodded. 'Yep, we've got restaurants to eat, scratch and win at. I already have a list of where the major prizes have been won so far. There's one in Brisbane at Redcliffe, one down at the Gold Coast, and the other in Melbourne, near St Kilda.'

Rose looked at Nic. 'Just how many Facebook friends have you got? Surely they couldn't all know about the competition?'

Nic smiled. 'Chewy has been running a search programme. It picks up any 'winner' words, or 'look at what I just won', that sort of thing. You would be surprised how many people start a Facebook post with 'winner, winner chicken dinner' even if it is just meeting a prospective beau for the first time.'

Rose went through the prize list. 'So, there are five cars worth a total of a hundred thousand, a couple of overseas holidays worth around ten thousand each, and various gift vouchers. All up, around two hundred thousand in prizes, including the free meals they are giving away. So, where's the scam?'

Nic pulled out another page; it showed that three cars and one overseas holiday had already been claimed. 'The investigation had shown the prizes so far were awarded to people who appear to be distantly related, which makes it too random to be random.'

Rose took a sip of her chardonnay and a bite of pizza, put a slice for Dog on a plate, and placed it onto the decking. Rose shook her head. 'Surely it can't be that easy. Maybe we ring the winners and ask them to give up the prizes?'

'Not sure yet. The game's afoot, a leg and maybe even a toe, so let's get this show on the road.'

'OK then ', Nic of Time, who knows how to rhyme', who's going where, when, and how?'

'I'll get Chewy to look into the one in St Kilda if Dee-Dee and Seiko head up to Redcliffe when they can, and Rose and I will go down to Mermaid Beach to see if they're real. I know The Gold Coast is aptly named, and Rainbow Beach, on the border, is too, but I don't understand why there is a nearby sub-urb called Labrador, although the weather down there gets ruff, ruff, woof, woof.'

Dog looked up at him and put one of his massive paws onto Nic's mouth.

'Nic.'

'Yes, Rose.' Dog suddenly jumped off his lap, so Nic stood and brushed fur from his jeans. 'Even Dog is getting tired of your Dad jokes.'

Nic smiled and leaned down to pat Dog on his head. 'Good Dog. Anyway, I've got other things to do, guys. Chewy is doing a bit of data mining so we can understand what's going on with the restaurant staff. He's also managed to track down the guy trying to sell our little doggy friend, so he's sending the bloodhounds around to leave a calling card on the front lawn if they're not home.'

Rose shook her head again. 'Oh, another thing. I've got a date next week.'

Nic stopped and turned around. 'What? Tell me more, Rose. I thought I kept you too busy to find time for all the mushy stuff.'

Rose smiled at his comment. 'Well, it's a blind date. Sandy organised it for me from Adelaide.'

'So, you're leaving me alone to go back down for a weekend without me?'

Dee-Dee looked at him. 'Hey, that's not fair. I'm still here.'

'Yep, but you spend too much time solving crimes with Seiko, not with me.'

'True, the life of a ninja sister super sleuth is never dull.'

'Tell me about it.' Nic broke into the Billy Joel song, but suddenly, Goliath started howling, so he stopped. 'Wow, I didn't expect such a little dog could make such an awful noise.'

Rose looked at him. 'He was singing Nic, but at least *he* was in tune.'

Nic continued. 'Anyway, Chewy's found a genealogy app. All the winners are from the same family, albeit very distantly. It's amazing what a few clicks here and there appear on those apps.'

Nic brought up a multi-linked 'family tree' on his phone, and after realising the screen was too small for the best vision, they relocated to the lounge room. He logged in and started scrolling across the tabs.

Rose noticed a name. 'Hey, stop. Who is that guy?'

Nic hovered over the name. 'Why?'

'That's the name of the guy I'm having lunch with next Friday. Amante Teleios. Sandy has set me up with him.'

'OK, but how did Sandy get onto him?'

'She'd been doing the rounds at the restaurant chain in Adelaide, and this guy kept showing up. So, she started up a conversation, and it turns out he's the National Marketing Manager for the restaurant chain. He's coming to Brisbane for a new store launch.'

'OK, but how did he hook up with you?'

'He uses the Vita Brevis dating app and likes to meet up with like-minded people whenever he returns to the city for a visit. Sandy overheard all this and sent off a 'like' thing, so we are meeting.

'I didn't think you were still using it, well, not since you met me anyway.'

'I like to keep my options open, Nic.'

'But...um...I've made some changes to your profile page.'

Rose nodded. 'Yes, we know, so we changed it back and added some other restaurant references, some foodstuff, and some other great stuff about me. Oh, and once we changed my name, he took the bait.'

'So, what should we call you, Rose?'

'Rosemary Plant.'

Dee-Dee looked at her. 'That's ridiculous.'

'Not really. He's a massive Led Zeppelin fan, so when you click on my profile, their song, 'Stairway to Heaven', starts up, and as Robert Plant was the band's lead singer, I hinted I could be related. I haven't checked him out yet, but Sandy reckons he's not too shabby.

Nic looked at her. 'So, you're scamming him?'

'I know how cool. Right?'

'Sort of, but be careful you don't know who, what, where and how. We only know why at this stage.'

'So, what's the why?'

'The 'why' is the reason for getting access to the prizes.'

Rose looked at him. 'Surely, people go for the food, drinks, and atmosphere first, and any marketing prize is just a ploy to get them back in again. You never hear of people winning these things, generally, they don't advertise a win. Otherwise, the winner gets a knock on the door, then a knock on the head, and the car or whatever winnings get stolen.'

'So true, Rose.'

Nic set the search 'Linked In' and located a photo of Amante Teleios. It showed a man around forty years old with the aura of a typecast Hollywood Prince: tall, dark, and extremely good-looking. Dee-Dee smiled at the picture. 'Whoa. Be careful with that one, Rose. He's up there with the beautiful people who only breathe the rarefied air.'

'That's OK Dee-Dee. I've been around Nic for a while.'

Nic laughed. 'Wow, that's the nicest thing you've said about me.'

'I was referring to your handsome French mate, Benoit Trudeau, and your ex-girlfriend's husband, the spectacular Dr Gabriel Goodenough.'

Nic nodded. 'Yep, I knew that. Anyway, I suggest we start looking into this stuff. Rose and I will spend a few days in my sister's place at Sanctuary Cove, checking out the restaurant at Mermaid Beach. Surf and sun might be on the agenda, too. A tough gig, but someone has to do it.'

Rose looked at him. 'I thought the house had been sold?'

'Yep, but there's a six-month settlement before exchanging titles. As long as we leave it tidy, it will be OK.'

Rose looked at him again. 'So, where will you be sleeping?'

'Nope, in a bunk bed in the children's room with Uncle Grumpy-Pants.'

'I'll bring my pliers and torture equipment to learn more from him about the enigma known to us as Nic Thorn.'

Dee-Dee looked over to Rose. 'You know he's not Nic's Uncle, right?'

Nic smiled. 'Yep, he's my Lawyer. I'll get Chewy to check out the St Kilda winner.' Nic mock saluted then looked around for Dog for one last pat on the head, but the cat was too busy finishing off his pizza and everyone else's.

CHAPTER 12

The following afternoon, Nic was leaning against his white Mustang waiting for Rose. Dave, the neighbour, and Goliath, the dog, had wandered over. 'Hey Nic, stealing Rose again, or have you come for your Dog fix?'

The little dog woofed a polite hello, so Nic leaned down to shake the dog's paw. 'And a good morning to you too, Goliath. Thanks for looking after the cat, the house, and all the precious stuff inside. I have taken them away a lot since I started...taking them away a lot.'

Dave nodded. 'It's all good, mate. I haven't seen Sandy around. Is she still in Adelaide?'

'Yep, she's down there staying with her Father, something about a parole hearing for her ex.'

'OK. You know about that too?'

'Yep, I've got contacts in high places. She won't have anything to worry about as my friend will ensure the guy doesn't see the light of day for quite a while.'

Dave continued: 'Well, they recently discovered a box of paintings and prints in the back seat of Uncle Albert's Jensen Interceptor that Rose sold recently. We assume the paintings were his too.'

Nic nodded. 'Uncle Albert liked to dabble in the arty stuff himself.'

Dave agreed. 'Yep, dabble was the word. He'd brush over the paint strokes with polyurethane to make the brush strokes appear legitimate in certain light. He never sold any, so I guess it was just an amusement for him.'

Nic nodded again, and they watched Rose make her way out of the house. Dog bounded along behind her and headed straight towards him. Dave looked at the cat. 'I've got this,' He pulled a giant dog biscuit from his pocket and threw it over Dog's head. The cat stopped to watch the airborne missile, then looked back at Nic and continued towards him.

'Wow, he must like you.'

'It's the 'bro code', mate. Living with two women as he does, Dog needs some man time. I lived on a farm with two sisters, and my father was working away, so I spent time with the Border Collies.'

Nic leant down, patted Dog on the head and looked to Rose. 'Your turn.'

Rose ignored him and climbed into the car, dropping her overnight bag onto the back seat. 'OK, Nic, let's get this show on the road. I chatted with Chewy and he's emailing me some background stuff about the Teleios Group.'

They said goodbyes and headed for the Gold Coast, which is about two hours drive away. Nic locked into the car's cruise control. 'Wow, so the reporting lines have changed. I'm not sure about that.'

Rose was about to respond when her phone chimed, so she opened the email and read it. 'Now that's interesting.'

'Tell me more, Rose. I'm a need-to-know person; hang on, I'm a have-to-know person. It's what I do.'

Rose continued. 'Well, someone has already won two cars, and they have already been sold on Gumtree. That means a quick rollover for cash in a few days of being awarded to the winners. There's also evidence a couple of the ten thousand dollar vouchers have been converted to cash. I estimate the prizes have been converted into a hundred thousand so far, but Chewy hasn't tracked down where the funds have ended up. He's just been able to trace the Vehicle Identification Number on the cars and the voucher serial numbers.'

Nic nodded. 'OK, that's a good start. It should be easy to track down the deposits into a Bank Account. If not, there is a large pile of cash to hide under someone's bed, making for one lumpy slumber.'

Rose shook her head. 'Tell me about Sandy and her thing going on in Adelaide with the parole hearing and her ex.'

He looked over. 'So what makes you think I know about that?'

'Um....well, remember that we ate at that fancy restaurant in Adelaide, and you met Robb Fraser for the first time, and then you were inspired to make a late-night visit to the South Australian Police Commissioner for some background on Sandy's past.'

'Um... yourself. How do you know about that, too?'

'Chewy told me.'

'First, he tells you his real name, then he tells you about my secret spying stuff.'

'Yep, he's leaking like a fish in a sieve.'

'I must be losing my superpower of superintelligence and my super influence over him.'

'Maybe it's more about he trusts me more as I get closer to the sun.'

'Yep, to that too. I'll hear back from Robb or Gerry, but I suspect the guy won't see the light of day for a while. He's a third of the way through the prison sentence, and there are no grounds for early parole. Sandy was fortunate that she didn't....' Nic paused, so Rose interrupted him. 'Please don't go there. Tell me something nice instead.'

'Well, Uncle Grumpy-Pants likes you, and he's impressed that you've managed to keep me under control. Oh, and I'll even let you know his real name.'

'Nope, it's OK. The less I know, the less I know, you know.'

Nic nodded. 'Gee, and he says you're getting good at this investigation stuff.'

They drove silently and, around two hours later, arrived at the Sanctuary Cove property. Uncle Grumpy-Pants let them through the gates. 'Nic, you're late, making me more grumpy than usual. Hello Rose, nice to see you again, and I suddenly feel much happier. Hopefully, we can get to know each other better this time.' Nic went to drive into the garage. 'Sorry, Nic, your little pony is not going in there. I've just spent an hour vacuuming the floor.' Nic pulled the car to a stop and climbed out. 'Can I still have my birthday party here next week?'

Rose looked at him. 'I thought you were born in October?'

'Oh, I forgot. Maybe we can have your birthday party here instead? I'll provide the cake.'

'Mine's in December.'

'Crap, I'm getting too old to do parties anyway.'

Uncle G-P then led them inside and directed them to the bedrooms. 'Rose, you're in the Master Suite. It's got its own bathroom and a lovely view of the water.' Rose headed off, dropped her bag into the room, and checked out the bathroom with the view. The shower alcove was an enclosed glass booth with access to the outside deck via another door, so basically, you were showering outside. Rose wondered how the whole exposure thing worked, so she turned the shower taps on, and the glass walls became opaque. 'I can do this.'

Rose showered, changed clothes, and met the others in the kitchen.

Nic looked at her. 'We heard the shower running, so you worked out the nudie avoidance shower peek show.'

Rose smiles. 'Yes, a simple case of deductive reasoning. I'm getting good at that, apparently.'

Nic nodded. 'Good to know. So now we're heading down to Mermaid Beach to check out the restaurant. I'll have you back in Brisbane for lunch with Amante on Friday at his new Hamilton restaurant. Dee-Dee and I will be there to monitor things, just in case. You don't need to interact with us or anything. We'll just be around.'

'Don't you trust me to handle him?'

'It's not that. It's just that we don't know who's who in the zoo as yet. The more we watch, the more or less we won't have to keep an eye on things.'

In the meantime, Uncle G-P was busying himself in the kitchen preparing the meal. Rose was mesmerised by the performance, whenever an item was removed from the cupboard or bench, it was quickly washed, dried, and returned. It was like watching a robot.

Nic noticed her watching. 'See, you made fun of me when I did that at your parent's place with the Mason jar and the Lisianthus. The apple doesn't fall far from the tree, does it?'

'Apparently, you're not related to him.'

'Oh yeah, I forgot that too.'

'Well, will you tell me how you know Uncle Grumpy-Pants then?'

'Maybe one day, and when the need arises, I'll introduce you to all the rest of my family.'

'I'll look forward to that. I already know your sister, Nicole, lives in Murrayville, and both of your parents are still alive. Is there someone else I need to meet? I can't possibly know anyone else until someone dies.'

Uncle G-P then strolled with the lunch and carefully placed it on the dining table, but not before wiping it over and putting placemats down. 'I can't do much more of this cleaning stuff, Nic; it's driving me crazy.'

'Well, you could leave it all until we return to Brisbane.'

'But what will I do to keep busy?'

'Have you cleaned the pool yet?'

'Yes, but I haven't vacuumed it. I don't think the Wet and Dry Vacuum cleaners are made to work underwater, are they?'

Rose looked at him. 'Just how long have you known Nic?'

Nic looked over to her. 'Well, he knows I used to ride a Harley but had to sell it when I was going out with Xanthe. Her parents thought I looked too much like a rebel with a cause, and she was the cause.'

Rose shook her head in dismay. 'Are we going to the restaurant then?'

Nic nodded. 'Yep, and are you up for a bit of surfing?'

Uncle G-P looked at them. 'I'll be into that, and I even know a guy who can lend us some boards for a couple of hours.'

He opened his phone and pressed a couple of buttons. 'Done.'

The front doorbell chimed, and he walked over to the video vision. 'It's the Dude from next door, so we've got the nod. He'll give us ten, and we'll meet outside.'

Rose looked at him. 'That was quick.'

'Yes, he's a Sup rider and keeps his surf gear on hand so we can go for a surf after lunch every day. It's part of the routine of what we retirees do.'

'So you're retired then, G-P? Retired from what exactly?'

'Um...over to you, Nic.'

Nic considered his response. 'OK, I will let you further into the inner sanctum of the Thorn family. I hope you're ready. We are all illegal aliens from Krypton, and a meteor destroyed our planet. We were sent to Earth to save the world from scammers.'

Rose shook her head. 'I don't think so, as you're not faster than a speeding bullet. I've seen you run.'

'Would you believe we are stranded here and looking for our way home? If only we could find a phone.'

'E.T. did that already, and he went back. So, there's hope for you.'

'True. Anyway, get your kit on or off, whatever suits your surfing style, and we'll go and catch some waves. The best place is Greenmount, and we can do the restaurant on the way back this afternoon.'

Rose went to her room to change.

G-P was still wiping down the kitchen surfaces. 'Does she surf?'

'I've no idea. Rose doesn't like getting wet so that it could get interesting.'

G-P nodded. 'It's just like a giant soggy bucking bronco that likes to dump water on your head, but other than that, it's quite good fun.'

Rose returned after about five minutes, still dressed in the same clothes. 'It's been a few years since I rode the waves, so hopefully, I can remember. The surf report says two to three-metre swell. There's probably a surfing competition down there too. It might be busy.'

Nic nodded. 'It's the Gold Coast. The fifty kilometres of the beach is one long surfing completion, just for the space on the waves.'

The group went outside and was introduced to the neighbour. His ride was a Black Toyota Hilux, with two stand-up paddle boards clamped onto the roof racks and another eight surfboards in the rear tray. 'Hi, I'm the Dude from next door. You must be Gomez and Morticia. Uncle Fester has told me so little about you.'

Uncle G-P leaned over towards Nic and Rose. 'I told him we're the Addams Family and are on holiday from the United States. I call him 'The Dude.' We discuss nothing other than surfing, life, and everything else.'

They climbed into the truck and headed off. 'So Fester, how long have you left until the house settlement goes through?'

'Still a couple of weeks yet so that we can surf every day until then. I might even get the confidence to enter one of the competitions.'

Rose piped up. 'Been there, done that.'

Nic looked at her. 'When? That definitely wasn't on your dating app.'

The Dude called out from the front. 'Hey, most people lie on those dating things, Gomez. I'm listed as an ex-television star from a river town in South Australia who used to sail around the world in his yacht.'

Rose responded. 'I always wondered what happened to you. Are you one of the lost Leyland Brothers or the blonde bushy-haired dude who made those awesome adventure shows with the blonde shipmates in tow? His name was Alby something.'

'Your choice, Morticia. Have you surfed?'

'Yes, but I just got dumped too many times. Firstly, it was the waves, and then my boyfriends got annoyed with me after I'd won too many competitions. They didn't like me surfing better than them. It's been a while, though.'

About an hour later, The Dude guided the Hilux into a car space, and they unloaded all the boards. 'This one will suit you, young lady. It's got four fins, so you'll get good control. For you, Gomez, stick to two. Fester, and I will take the SUPs.'

They headed to the beach, and The Dude handed over a spray can for waxing the boards. 'Try this stuff, guys. It's my invention. I've been working on it for years. I used to be a biochemist in my younger days, and it saves us stealing all the beeswax from the beehives.'

Several surfers were already on the water, so they looked for a quieter place to enter. The Dude and Fester went in the water first and were well out before they realised the others were not following. Fester caught a wave, rode it back and glided up to them. 'What's up, guys? The water's too cold for you?'

Rose responded first. 'No, it's just once I get out there, I've got...well, I'm a goofy footer, and there are people around that I recognise from about fifteen years ago when I was doing the circuit.'

The Dude nodded. 'Well, keep your head down and your board up. No one will notice. Just don't do anything special. They're too busy catching their rides.'

Nic looked at her. 'Just how good were you?'

Rose unzipped her windbreaker revealing a tight-fitting multicoloured rashie. The front was decorated with several surfing sponsorship patches and on the back it read: "QLD U17 Titles-Palmer." Rose hand-pressed at the creases. 'It used to be a little looser. I won a few national titles in the day, but it all fell in a hole when Father stepped in and told me to stop surfing and get a real job. He then informed me I needed to marry the stupid id-iot, Michael the Gormless.'

They paddled out into the waves, and Rose re-lied on her muscle memory for moves she had done so well years before, cutting through the waves, curling, flipping on the crests and even managing a 180° turn. Nic, in the meantime, was floating on his board, not catching anything. Rose caught another wave and rode it into shore, then returned and paddled up to him. 'So, surfing is not your thing, Nic?' He looked over at her. 'It used to be.'

They stayed in the water for two hours, and eventually, The Dude and G-P decided to call it a day as the hordes began to arrive, and it was get-ting quite congested. Rose was catching her last wave when suddenly a rider cut in front but she skilfully slowed down to let him through and as he dropped in, he yelled out: 'Get off my ride.'

Rose mock-saluted and executed a complete 180° turn to avoid him, but he lost his balance and the wave dumped him. He was waiting on the shore when she rode the wave in. Rose looked at him. 'Do I know you?'

The surfer responded. 'Nope, but I've been watching you.' He then poked his forefinger into her shoulder and twisted at the fabric. 'These were awarded at the State Championships in the late nineties. Where did you get it?'

Rose shrugged. 'I used to surf a bit in my younger days. I did the circuits here at the Goldy and Bells Beach but my parents told me I had to focus my energies elsewhere.' The surfer glared at her. 'Next time I won't be so nice. Don't drop in on me.' He then turned and walked away.

Meantime, Nic, G-P and The Dude ambled over. 'Everything good here, Morticia?' Rose pushed her board into the sand. 'Yep, the guy was selling me the big wave stuff. You know, the rush of adrenalin from the adventures that are missing in my life now.'

The group returned to the truck, loaded the boards, showered at a nearby facility, changed into their civvies and were now seated at the restaurant. Nic called the waiter over. 'I've heard there's a scratch-and-win completion being offered here, but I can't see any marketing. We're up from interstate and only came to see if we can grab a prize.'

'I'm sorry, Sir, it has been temporarily suspended. A few restaurants are still running with it back in Brisbane if you're heading up that way.'

Nic nodded. 'Thanks. So what's good to eat here then?'

'Everything is perfect, and as they say in Greek, it's 'teleios.'' They ordered four of the Greek share plates, including dolmades, moussaka, kokolythokeftedes, pieces of bread and olives and soon desert was being served with strong Loumidis coffees and ouzo.

About three hours later, the group returned to Sanctuary Cove where they shared a six-pack of Mythos beer. Surfing was discussed, and Nic managed to locate a vision of Rose surfing from the late nineties. The Dude finally left, and Nic made a coffee for Rose. 'I thought you don't like to get wet?'

'Well, some of us have our secrets to keep. Don't we, like who is Uncle Grumpy-Pants?' Nic ignored the question and decided to call Chewy for an update on the St Kilda investigation. The phone was put on speaker. 'Yo bro, what you know? You're on speaker.' 'Yo bros, and bro-esses. It's colder than a mother-in-law's kiss down here. I'm sitting on the St Kilda jetty, and everyone's wandering around dressed in penguin suits. It's just like a high school formal.'

Nic shook his head at the comment. 'I think they are penguins, mate.'

Chewy continued: 'Hey, you're right. Anyway, nothing much is happening. I've been to the restaurant several times but haven't worked out if any of these guys are involved. I'll visit the guy that sold the car and see what's what.'

Rose interjected. 'How are you going to do that? Just knock on the door and ask them to give up the information?'

Chewy went quiet for a moment. 'I was going to try that, but I think I'll try the old 'there's a problem with your paperwork' trick. I'll wear a nice black hat and a nice black suit, and pretend I'm from the nice Tax Office. Then I'll visit the guy that bought the car and see what's what.'

Nic nodded. 'That's a lot of what's what, Chewy.'

'I know, but I'll have my sidekick to kick anyone who troubles me.' Rose leaned towards the phone. 'I thought you were Tonto, and Nic was your only Lone Ranger?'

'Nope, I'm flexible like that and I can inter-change my superhero loyalties. This time, I've elected to use Driver Two. He likes to be invisible just like his brother.' Nic was about to finalise the call when Chewy continued. 'Oh, there is one thing I've picked up at the restaurant. The inventory keeps getting messed up, and the kitchen staff get a bit loud when they discover the fish stock has gone missing.'

Nic leaned towards the phone again. 'Make sure they check for any seals loitering around the fridges. The restaurant is close to the beach, you know.'

They disconnected the call, and Nic rang Dee-Dee for an update on their investigation at the Redcliffe site. 'Hi, Dee-Dee. Have you found anything?'

Dee-Dee responded. 'Yes. I've found a Gumtree ad for a travel voucher being for sale. The guy selling it needed the money to pay for an operation for his grandmother. It was quite a good pitch, and he was convincing. I've managed to talk him down to eight thousand dollars. He sent me a copy to prove it was legitimate. Seiko did a Police check and confirmed it was from the restaurant group. We're on our way there now to collect it.'

'Is Seiko with you?'

'Yes, but don't worry, we won't buy it. Seiko will bring out the Police Badge, and we will retain it as evidence.'

Nic nodded. 'That sounds like a plan. Just be careful anyway. Don't go inside the house. You know the drill.' Nic disconnected and moved outside to join G-P and Rose, enjoying the sunset over the water.

Rose stood up and walked over to the swimming pool. 'This is weird, Nic, when we travel to Adelaide, the sun sets over the sea and rises over the hills. Here, it rises over the sea and sets over the hills.'

G-P responded quietly. 'And when you live in Antarctica, you pray for a sunrise and sunset.' Rose looked at him, and Nic shook his head. 'Look at what you've done now, G-P, Rose will want you to spill all your family secrets.'

G-P suddenly stood up and deliberately spilled his wine on his pants. 'Oops. I've spilled my wine. I need to change my clothes.' He rushed inside, and Nic's phone rang again. 'Yo, Dee-Dee, what's up?'

Dee-Dee was whispering. 'We're in a little trouble, Nic. We thought this guy was checked out. Seiko is ... we thought he was by himself, but he's here with about ten friends. They're having a party. They won't let us go until we hand over the cash, and we won't do that without the voucher. They insisted on us coming around the back and joining the party. We thought it ....would be....didn't go inside.'

Nic responded quickly. 'Where's Seiko?'

'They have her...she's standing by the roasting lamb...on a spit.....She's not going to pull out her badge. It might get messy. I've managed to sneak away and am hiding inside the house.'

'I'll get you out. Forget the voucher. Give me ten.' Nic disconnected. 'G-P, can you get out here, please? We need to use ....' He looked over to Rose. 'We need some of your people.'

G-P stepped from the house wiping his hands on a dishcloth. 'What's up, Nic? I was dusting the pelmets.' Nic stood up. 'Who do you know at Redcliffe? Dee-Dee and Seiko have sort of ...well, we don't know, but I need to get them to safety.'

'Can we use the Police?'

'Seiko is the Police.'

'Oh, sorry, I forgot. Whereabouts are they located in Redcliffe?'

'By the Golf Course. The property backs onto the eighteenth hole.'

'OK. I'll call the club.'

Rose looked at him. 'It's well past eight; nobody will be playing this time of night.'

'Nope, but there'll be people in the bar, and they have a lot of trouble with possums this time of year. Club members go on possum patrols every Saturday night to catch, relocate, and release. Occasionally, they might venture into someone's backyard to catch and release something bigger.'

Rose nodded. 'And you can organise that?'

Nic looked at her. 'Where do you think I learnt my trade? Doing, knowing, and getting stuff done is part of his forte, too. We are the possum people. You never know where we might be needed to play possum.'

G-P moved away, made a phone call, and returned ten minutes later. 'They're safe.' Nic nodded. 'Wow, that was quick. What happened? Did all the possums get rescued?'

'Not quite. When I rang Dee-Dee to let her know what was about to happen, she told me they'd already left. The Fire Brigade had turned up as the smoke detectors went off inside the house. Dee-Dee told the group that someone had burnt the roast potatoes left in the oven.'

Rose shook her head. 'Didn't they realise the potatoes were likely being cooked with the lamb spit?'

G-P looked at her. 'You've been around Nic too long. Sometimes you can see the wolf, but they're not dressed in sheep's clothing.'

CHAPTER 13

The following day, Nic and Rose drove up to Brisbane for Rose's luncheon with Amante Teleios. To save time, they went directly to the restaurant. Dee-Dee was already there, having scoped out the site. G-P and Rose headed off, and Nic turned to Dee-Dee. 'What do you know so far?'

Dee-Dee leaned toward him. 'Well, the Brisbane Head Office of the Teleios Group is upstairs on the mezzanine floor and directly above the restaurant. It's adjacent to the cinemas. You take either the stairs or the elevator. There's some minor refurbishing happening up there, too. They've fitted it out for new offices, so it's a little untidy. They have set party stuff for the children in the foyer on the ground floor. Face painting, an inflated jumping castle, that sort of thing, and pony rides are in the carpark. It's the grand opening of the new 'Teleios at Hamilton.''

Nic nodded. 'OK, anything else?'

'Yep, this one is 'owner operated' by Ivan Teleios, and there's a rumour that they call him 'Ivan the T' after that nasty Russian Czar. This guy has a bit of a temper, especially if all his ducks aren't in a row.' Nic considered for a moment. 'Did you manage to find out anything more about Amante Teleios?'

Dee-Dee continued: 'Nope, he seems pretty clean so far. He's tied up with four of the restaurants directly, and there are about eighty-five across Australia. Most are under a franchise agreement including this one here. They have plans to open another five by the end of the year. It must be a massive drain on cash flow. The new restaurants don't turn a profit until all the setup costs are added in.'

'OK, so what's the play here?'

'I've booked a table to be as close as we can to Rose, and we'll try and get access to Amante's phone so we can clone it, then I'll send it to Chewy to have a look.'

'Sounds like a plan. What about Uncle G-P?'

Nic nodded. 'He'll be around, but just not in the restaurant. I think he can handle himself if needed.'

'I think so too. Rose is due to meet with Amante in half an hour. Is there anything else I need to be aware of?'

'Nope, apart from when's lunch. I'm hungry.'

Nic and Dee-Dee headed toward the restaurant and were seated directly behind Rose. And Amante was not yet there. Rose acknowledged them whilst busy reading the menu and looked up when she felt a presence close to the table. The man exuded an aura of quiet style and confidence.

'Are you Rozzemary Plant? Your profile itz not, well, you are much more. I am Amante Teleios. Welcome.'

Rose stood up and allowed the man to kiss her hand lightly. 'Yes, I am Rosemary. Is this your restaurant? Is it far from home?' Amante smiled. 'My home iz where my heart iz, and my breath, it iz taken away with your beauty, Rozzemary.'

Nic had his back to Rose and was listening intently to the banter. 'Boy, Dee-Dee, he can't be real, although he does remind me of a young Antonio Banderas when he did the Zorro movie in the late '90s.'

Dee-Dee whispered: 'Oh no, that's all him, but we'll need a distraction to get to his phone. He doesn't allow the bulk of a phone or a wallet in his pants to affect the suit's lines, so I assume they're in his jacket pocket. Most likely the left side, as he's right-handed.'

'OK, how do we get him to take it off?'

'By turning the temperature up in the restaurant. I made sure that he was sitting directly under an air-conditioning vent. Give it a couple of minutes.' Dee-Dee removed a remote control from her handbag and pointed it towards the infrared plate under the unit, and after a couple of clicks, the temperature had increased by fifteen degrees. The heated air was now cascading over all of them.

Amante was engrossed in a conversation with Rose, so Nic again leaned towards De-Dee. 'I think we need to make something happen a bit quicker.' He then stood up and, as he did so, slid his chair into the back of Rose's. 'I'm so sorry; it's just getting warm here. I'm going to remove my dinner jacket.'

Fortunately, this was enough to distract Amante from the intensity of the conversation, and Rose took the prompt and stood up to do the same thing. 'Do you mind, Amante? I think I'm getting a little warm, too.'

Armante nodded. 'Oh yez, Rozzemary. It iz the Brizbane weather.'

Amante stood up, and Rose assisted him in removing his jacket, then she placed it over the chair behind *her*, however, as he was about to sit back down, Ivan the T came out from a rear storage area and beckoned him to follow him to the kitchen. 'I'm zo zorry Rozzemary. It is my couzin. It appears that I have been summoned.'

In the meantime, Dee-Dee and Nic had started a minor argument that ended in Dee-Dee throwing a pitcher of water at him. Nic ducked out of the way, and the water drenched Amante's coat on the rear of Rose's chair. Rose realised this was an opportunity to get to the phone, so she raised the coat from the back of the chair and started wiping the excess water. At the same time, Nic slipped her the cloning equipment, and then Dee-Dee stormed out of the restaurant. Nic waited a couple of minutes, settled the bill, and left.

Amante returned to the table and again apologised for the interruption. He then noticed that Rose was holding his jacket and phone. 'What haz happened, Rozzemary? My jacket looks wet. Is my phone OK?'

'I think so, the couple behind us argued. It got awkward; she asked him to marry her, and he laughed, so she threw the water pitcher at him. He ducked, and your jacket got wet.'

'Are you OK? I'll payz to have your outfit dry cleaned if you need.'

Ros shook her head. 'No, but thank you for the offer. It looks like you've got a busy day here today with the restaurant's opening, so if it's OK, I might leave now.'

'Thank you. I have much to do, and Ivan is not very happy. He thinkz that zomeone is watching him. He'z under a bit of strezz with all the restaurants we are opening. I told him that four in the same week iz too much.'

Rose hugged Amante and made her way out of the restaurant when Ivan stopped her from leaving. He looked at her sternly. 'You. Come with me,' and held her by the wrist to lead her up the nearby stairs. Rose considered crying out for help but decided it was not a good idea as he was one very grumpy, Ivan the Terrible.

As they reached the top of the stairs, Rose noticed Uncle Grumpy-Pants sitting on a chair over by the office. His head was bowed, and his hands were tethered to his thighs. 'Hiya Rose. I got caught snooping; sorry about that.' Ivan led her towards G-P, directing her to sit down alongside him. 'You are not a Rosemary Plant; you are Rose Palmer. My man at the beach he recognised you. What are you doing wanting with my cousin?'

'I'm no one. I don't know anything. He found me on a website. I've been having lunch, that's all.' Ivan glared at them. 'Mmm... so tell me about this man then? He's been watching me, and I don't like it.'

Rose tried to keep calm. 'He's my Uncle G-P....um Garry... Garry Pants. Are you OK, Garry?'

G-P raised his head. 'I've been better, Rose, thanks for asking. I'm a little tied up at the moment. Would you mind loosening these for me?' Rose noticed the black plastic ties around his wrists. 'Now, that's not nice, Ivan. Can I loosen them a bit, please?' Ivan looked at her and handed over a pair of pliers to sever the ties. Rose moved over, gathered another set from the table next to G-P, and helped G-P stand up, but Ivan growled at them when he sat back down.

'Hands behind you....'

They obeyed his instructions, then G-P held his arms behind him to allow Rose to re-attach the ties, but this time, whilst G-P was shielded from Ivan by her body, Rose shackled two onto his wrist, then used two additional ties to make a longer chain, which resulted in extending the length.

G-P nodded at her once it was done and folded the two longer links back into his palms. It was Rose's turn, and she sat down whilst Ivan tied her wrists. Ivan stepped away and pondered his options. He moved over towards the balcony, placed his hands on the railing and stood there with his back to them.

Rose leaned towards G-P. 'I think he's slightly angry, and his breathing is a little laboured. Do you think he'll turn green or anything like that?'

They watched Ivan a little more, and he eventually turned around. He looked at them, sighed, crossed his arms over his chest, took another deep breath and exhaled. 'Aaaarrgh.' He continued to remonstrate loudly, then looked around the construction site and moved towards a box of rolled cardboard.

Ivan picked a large one from the box, hefted it and went through a faux attack and defence routine. G-P looked at the makeshift weapon. 'Mmm, I think he may know Kendo, and it could get ugly, or we might get bored; card-board.'

Rose nodded. 'Wow, and he's quite good. There's quite an art to it, and speaking of art, are you hanging around with us for this thing that my Father is putting together at the Maritime Museum?'

G-P shook his head. 'I don't know yet. Nic told me the artwork is a bit suspect. How far have you looked into it?'

Rose shrugged.

Ivan glared at them; 'Stop talking,' then he continued with the Kendo routine, moving effortlessly from an attack into a defensive mode.

Rose was quite impressed. 'He doesn't say much, though, does he? Could a 'Mr Silent Type' be a new super-villain?'

Ivan sneered at them. 'I told you to stop talking.'

He headed towards them, wielding the makeshift weapon, when suddenly, the elevator chimed. The doors opened, and a man dressed in a black suit, wearing a black plastic bowler hat, holding a large black folded umbrella, stepped out, rolling the umbrella through his wrists ala 'Charlie Chapin' style.

'Hello, I'm a little lost. I'm here for the Mary Poppins reunion, and my umbrella won't open.'

Ivan looked at him suspiciously. 'I know who you are, Mr Nic Thorn. Go away.'

'Well, I'm here now, and it looks like I've stumbled into something nasty.'

Nic moved carefully towards him and nodded over to Rose and Uncle G-P. 'Hi, guys. I'll be your chosen superhero today if you like. Call me Mr Umbrella-Man.'

Ivan moved around the space. 'What are you on about?' Then he collected another solid rolled cardboard pipe, hefted it between his hands and manoeuvred himself around Nic. Ivan was now leaning back against the mezzanine rail.

Uncle G-P stood up, lengthened the four chains of the ties, and stepped through them so his hands were in front of him. Nic tossed the umbrella to him, which he caught quickly.

Ivan squared off against G-P. 'So, what will you do? Attack me with an umbrella?' He then dismissively turned away and looked down at the children's party happening below, and the others could see that he was trembling with frustration.

Rose took the opportunity to collect a solid iron pipe from underneath her seat and slid it between the folds of the closed umbrella.

Ivan had now turned back around, having decided his best defence would be an attack and lurched forward. Uncle G-P responded with 'En-garde' and held out the umbrella. Ivan parried, then raised his weapon above his head and crashed it onto the umbrella. Ivan's weapon broke in half.

Nic then lowered his shoulder, barged into Ivan, and together they tumbled over the balcony rail. Rose screamed, stood up, rushed over, looked down, and saw that Ivan and Nic had landed in the middle of the inflated jumping castle three metres below.

It was otherwise unoccupied, and they wrestled on the rubber mat.

Ivan was the first to move from the mattress and roll through an open screen. Nic tried to grab at his heels to prevent him from leaving but only managed to gather a shoe.

Ivan then left the restaurant and turned left to make his escape. Nic then bunted his way to the side of the inflatable pad and waited for Rose and Uncle G-P to join him downstairs. 'I don't think this is a Cinderella story as we already know who owns the other shoe. Spoiler alert.' He dropped the collected shoe just as Amante and some patrons came from the restaurant to see what the commotion was about. Rose came up to Nic and softly double-fisted him in the chest. 'Damn you, Nic. How did you know that was going to work? How did you know that there wouldn't be any children in there? How did you know you would even survive that fall?'

'Boy, you ask a lot of questions.'

'Well, that was a dangerous move, even for you.'

Nic smiled. 'It was all rehearsed. That's why G-P was up there, and I had all those cardboard cylinders left for Ivan and the metal pipe for you. We even put a label with instructions on it just in case.'

Rose carefully opened the dented umbrella, extracted the pipe, and looked for a label. There was one that read 'Caution. Do not open inside'.

Rose looked at Nic, and he shrugged his shoulders.

'Anyhow, how did you know Ivan would go up there?'

'We sent him a message that we'd discovered what he was up to and wanted our cut to keep it all quiet. I told him to meet with G-P up there.'

Amante came over, wanted to know what was happening, and held out his hand. 'I am Amante Teleios. I believe you are Nic Thornz?'

'Yes, and this is Rose Palmer and Uncle Grumpy-Pants. Two of my associates.'

Amante looked at Rose disappointedly, ignored Uncle G-P, and then back to Nic. 'So, what iz this all about, Mr Thorn? Iz Ivan involved?'

'Yes, unfortunately, Amante. It has to do with his cash flow. He'd realised he could get early access to the prizes, cash them in and pump money back into his new restaurants. We've tracked down who he used and followed the money trail. Most of it ended up back in his bank accounts.'

'Zo he's made money from us, to get money to make ourz a better business? It waz his idea for the competition in the first place. He could've zaid that he needed the money.'

Nic looked up at the balustrade and nodded. 'Well, you know what they say.....pride comes before a fall.'

Amante didn't quite understand what the comment meant, so he moved away to tend to the existing restaurant patrons. Most were still waiting for the next acrobatic performance on the jumping castle but were deflated as the air was extracted.

Dee-Dee then came back into the foyer. 'Sorry, Nic, I tried to follow him, but he jumped on one of the little horses and rode off into the sunset. I assume he's heading for the Hamilton Ferry to make his escape. He's gone.'

Nic shook his head. 'I suspect he'll be taking the next ferry, and unless he jumps off and swims to shore, he'll only get to the Eagle Street Pier in the city as it's the only ferry running at the moment. The Fraud Squad will catch up with him there. We timed it that way.'

Rose looked at him. 'How do you know he doesn't have a car parked at the Ferry Terminal or that he'll call an Uber?'

Nic opened his hand. 'I took his phone and car key after we landed in the jumping castle.'

In the meantime, Amante had corralled the restaurant staff and offered the remaining guests free pony rides and face painting as a goodwill gesture. Nic moved over to him.

'I guess that was the most exciting first date you've had for a while?'

Amante smiled. 'It doesn't count as a firzt date. Roze and I will be seeing each other again. She works for you. Is it OK?'

Nic leaned forward and then whispered. 'Yep, but please be careful with her. She is very...' Instead of completing his sentence, he saluted Amante, then moved outside to a waiting driver so their group could return to the city. As they climbed into the car, Rose looked at Nic. 'Just what did you say to Amante?'

Nic smiled. 'It's secret men's business, Rose.'

They decided to detour to collect Sandy from the airport, and on the way back into the city, Nic called Chewy to update him on the developments.

'The job is over unless you found something fishy in St Kilda?'

'Well, the fishy thing just turned out to be the sous-chef stealing the fish to feed the penguins, but it did explain why they kept waddling up to him every time he went on his meal breaks. He was like the St Kilda Pied Piper of Penguins.'

'What about the car thing?'

'Oh yeah. That's not so fishy. I watched the guy sell the car, and then another guy turned up an hour later and took the cash off him.'

'What did the guy look like?'

'Um....terrible. I've managed to take a couple of pictures of him. The guy was tall, dark, and ugly.'

Nic nodded. 'What time was that?'

'About twelve-thirty last night. I'm working on enhancing the pixels to get a better view.'

Nic nodded. 'That would most likely have been Ivan the Terrible. No wonder he looks terrible, as he was here in Brisbane to launch the opening of his restaurant. He must've caught the red-eye this morning.'

Around an hour later, Nic's crew were back at his apartment in South Bank. They were standing out on his balcony, bathing in the glory of having quietly solved another investigation and admiring the view of the Brisbane city lights.

Sandy sidled over to Rose. 'You know, Rose, I never suspected Amante would be involved.'

'Me either. Really, really, really good-looking people only ever steal hearts.'

CHAPTER 14

About a week later, Rose and Sandy had headed off on their early morning coffee and newspaper pilgrimage. Rose noticed a poster pinned against the wall. It advertised the Art Show and Shine Exhibition at the South Bank Maritime Museum. 'Well, that's our next little thing if we're not needed for Nic Thorn and Associates.'

They took their coffees and headed back home. 'It's in a week, but I'm sure Nic will find somewhere to go or something to look into to keep us busy. I'm surprised as we usually roll from one scam investigation to another.'

'It's all good. Anyway, they're working on something big. I've been getting snippets of info out of Chewy. They have around ten projects on the go at any one time, but it's only the bigger ones we get drawn into. The rest are solved by shifting the papers around the sandbox and smacking a few people on their noses.'

'So, what have you heard?'

'It's only early days, but some staff at one of the Big Four Banks have been implicated in an equipment leasing scam. It's something to do with the equipment inspection and paying over the money without checking things are above board.'

They stopped outside their house and saw that Dog was attempting to jump from the ground to capture a small twittering bird from a low-hanging tree branch. It wasn't working, and they could see the cat was getting frustrated.

'How often does that happen?'

'I think we feed him too much.'

'No, not the cat ... the Bank thing.'

Rose shrugged. 'About thirty years ago, there was a huge fraud involving the Victorian Safety Council. Chewy reckons that someone sticks their head up every ten years or so and tries to figure out how the bloke got away with it. That one involved hundreds of millions of dollars.'

'That sounds way above our pay grade.'

'Yes, so we might not be called up. Anyway, let's go in and see what we can do with that box of Uncle Albert's paintings we found in his car. Maybe Father can use some of them as they're all fakes or simple prints anyway.'

They went inside, pulled the box out of the wardrobe and spread the prints on the dining table. Sandy looked over the cache. 'Some of these have been painted over. Why was he doing that?'

'I have no idea. I've read that the art experts have a process called pentimento, but that's when the artist has made a mistake or didn't like where the hand or head was. Albert has painted red acrylic paint over this one. I assume he didn't the look of it.'

They looked at the collection and noticed one of the smaller ones fully signed, so Rose picked it up. 'This one looks real, as much as a fake can look real.'

Sandy nodded. 'Maybe that's one for the Art Show then.'

In the meantime, Dog had come inside and was making his way across the dining table, and they tried to tempt the eight-kilogram Dog off the table by throwing a stick of celery out to the back deck, but the cat just looked at them. Rose stood up. 'I guess Dog needs to be fed again' and topped up his bowl with kitty dins.

It was another warm, perfect blue sky day in Brisbane, and Sandy slowly sipped her coffee. 'I didn't hear you get in last night. How did your second date with Amante 'the seriously good looking' go?'

'Well, he's swamped now that Ivan the T had to take some personal time.'

'And?'

'Well, he likes his phone, and....I just felt guilty about Nic.'

'You and Nic, there is no guilt, Rose. We have that pact.'

'Yes, but it's more about the integrity of Nic Thorn and Associates. After the fifth time, Amante excused himself to take a call, I brought up the 'Teleios family tree' that Chewy had sent to my phone. The tentacles of the Teleios family number well into the forties, and that's just the ones that Chewy connected in one day. I realised that I can't get into anything whilst we're still involved in everything we're still involved in with Nic. Family protection is the NTA motto.'

'NTA?'

'Nic Thorn and Associates. After about fifteen minutes, I left, deleted Amante's phone number, and caught an Uber to Nic's warehouse at Bowen Hills. Dee-Dee, Seiko and Nic were working through the final Police brief on the Teleios Case. I left there at about eleven thirty. It won't be a formal Police matter as long as the family releases an apology in the local papers.'

Sandy smiled. 'Has Amante tried to contact you?'

'Nope, but he can't, as the phone number I provided him no longer exists. I also overheard him saying that he's heading off to Newcastle for the grand opening of another family restaurant, and as they say in the classics, a man's heart is through his stomach."

Sandy shook her head. 'Fair enough, but I do prefer the last line from 'Gone with the Wind' ...'Damn you, Nic."

Rose smiled. 'Not quite. It was 'after all, tomorrow is only a day away', but I think that could be from 'Annie'. I always get my musicals mixed up.

It must be something to do with all the hills being alive with the sound of music.'

Rose and Sandy watched Dog suddenly jump down from the papasan, and there was a soft cough at the top of the stairs. It was Nic. 'That's from the musical Annie. I thought you'd been studying up on all the pop culture and musical stuff?'

Rose nodded. 'Hey, I've already gone past The Byrds and the 'B's. Quick, ask me a question about 'A' and the Animals, but don't let me be misunderstood .'

Nic smiled. 'I like the sound of NTA. I'll Google it to see if it is already being used.' Nic started scrolling through his phone. 'Mmm...Nett Tangible Asset, National Testing Agency, Nice Tasty Apples, Nanoparticle Tracking Analysis, Nic Thorn and Associates.' They looked at him. 'I'm kidding. I didn't find anything. I was checking if you're both still listening to me.'

Rose nodded. 'Yes, Nic, we always do, except when you talk. What are we getting into now?'

'It's a bit quiet on the scamming front, so Chewy's been looking into the art thing that your Father is putting together. It's a lot more complicated than we thought. The people behind it can't be traced at the moment. They are cautious, and that's enough to be suspicious. If it all goes south, it means the only one left holding the burning candle at both ends would be the one and only Zachariah Palmer.'

'So what are we going to do?'

'How do you feel about painting the town red?'

'What's that supposed to mean?'

'Chewy sent me the details for the Art Show and Shine website. He is working on getting behind who has uploaded the website link, and the only name is Zachariah Palmer. That is odd, as I assume your Father is not a computer whiz or one to go at things alone?'

'Nope, as far as I know, and he's a hunt and peck typist too, single index finger thing.'

'That's what I thought. Also, it's only his name on the booking schedule for the Maritime Museum event. So it's all him, or he's being set up to take the fall.'

'What are we going to do?'

'I've arranged for a Jazz Band to play during the exhibition. It's a quartet of a wonderful group of guys.'

Rose shook her head, and Sandy smiled. 'And I assume you are the lead guitarist?'

'No, I'm playing the stand-up bass and use the Bowie thingy a bit too. No one will notice if I'm not keeping up. It's jazz, after all. The shark theme from 'Jaws' is my speciality. Dum-dum-da-dum.'

'Are you needing backup singers?'

'No, sorry, not this time. You'll be too busy being arty and won't have time to be jazzy.' Sandy nodded. 'If my friend Carly is singing and Sticks-Out plays the drums, who's making up the fourth?'

'Crusoe. He's always been eager to step out from behind the mixing desk and into the front of the house.'

'The last time we played with him, he was miming.'

'I know. Who says he won't be miming this time too?'

'We assume it will be live.'

'I know, and how cool will that be? As long as he doesn't sing, we'll be OK. He's been having singing lessons, but he still sounds like that penguin from Happy Feet. He's good at impersonations and does a good job of imitating Bob Dylan and Ringo Starr. Not at the same time, though.'

Rose smiled. 'Well, if he can sing whilst driving a Yellow Submarine whilst blowing in the wind, it should be OK.'

'Wow, you have picked up some more music stuff.'

'Yep. I'm now up to the 'D's, at least. Unfortunately, I'm going by stage names and not real names, and as Zimmerman is Bob Dylan's real last name, I could have skipped right to the end of the alphabet.'

Nic smiled. 'Oh, by the way, Chewy managed to track down the scammer pretending to sell Dave's little teacup dog. The IP address was eventually traced and matched, so we organised someone to visit him. He decided that taking the ad down was in his best interest.

'Where was the guy based? Somewhere around Brisbane?'

Nic shook his head. 'Not quite, and that's why it took so long. The guy lived on a boat moored on the Brisbane River here at West End for a while. He's spent his life sailing around Australia, taking pictures of animals and things to claim they are his and selling them. Dog was his downfall.'

Sandy nodded. 'Where did the Police catch up with him?'

Nic nodded. 'In old Hobart Town, Tasmania. He'd just completed editing his vision of his last Sydney to Hobart Yacht race, then sent the up-loaded link to all and sundry and because of the worm Chewy had attached to the Rose Gallery of Modern Art file, we finally got a match.'

'He confessed?'

'Yep, and agreed to stop his wickedly wacky ways.'

'Just like that?'

'No, unfortunately not. Chewy has already tracked a file of him trying to sell a Tasmanian devil. Each time he does that, anyone answering his ad gets a prompt that it's likely a scam. He doesn't know about it, as we send it back through Gumtree's website. They don't quite have the same sophisticated systems as we have access to, but they don't mind.'

Rose nodded. 'OK then, we've got about a week before Dad starts this art thing. What do you need us to do?'

'Let's go through the box of paintings you've got here to see if we can use anything.'

Rose headed back inside, and Sandy took a moment with Nic.

'You almost lost her. Amante might have swept her off her feet.'

'I know. Luckily, I hid all the brooms.'

Rose returned, put the box on the table, and Nic moved to flick through them, but Sandy slapped his hand away. 'They are treasures, so you can't put your grubby fingers on them. We have to use gloves.' Sandy leaned into the box, retrieved a pair of long silk gloves, handed one to Rose, and pulled on the other.

'Damn you guys, there's only two gloves, so I brought my own.' Nice placed his hand into his jacket pocket and pulled out his pair. They were fingerless, finely crocheted and very delicate.

Rose looked at him. 'Let me guess; you stole them from your mother?'

'Nope, your mother. I was shopping for a present for Mother's Day and ran into Jana at the shop of the Embroiders Guild in Hamilton. We started talking about life, stuff, and you, and then I mentioned I needed something nice for my mother, and she handed me these. Do you like them?'

Nic held up his hands and fluttered his fingers.

'They're OK. They make your fingers look fat and are girly but otherwise OK.'

'She bought them for you. I told her I would take them off her hands, so to speak.'

'In that case, get your grubby fingers out of them.' Nic nodded, licked his fingertips, cracked his knuckles, pulled the gloves off and put them on the table. Rose sighed and pulled the first painting out to carefully place it on the table.

Nic leaned over it, rubbed his chin, and rubbed Dog's head. 'So what do you think?' He held it up. Dog looked at it, and the cat then licked its paw. 'Nope, Dog doesn't like that one. Either do I, and I think Dog has a good eye for art.'

'It's upside down.'

Nic looked at it. 'Yep, I know that. Next.'

The art pieces were revealed one by one until one was left. 'So, can you tell the difference between real and fake?'

Nic looked at Sandy. 'Yep, I think so. Hit me, baby one more time.'

Dog then started clawing at Nic's legs, and once an eight-kilogram cat does that, you have to obey. 'Oh, that's nice. I think he wants me to stay.'

Rose pulled the last painting out. It was not much bigger than an A4 page, and Nic smiled. 'Dog likes it, as he's stopped washing. It's signed, too.' Nic held the picture by the frame and moved it toward better light for a closer inspection. 'I would say this could be real. It's signed, but I can't make the name.'

Nic pulled his phone from his pocket and attached a small lens to the camera to look at the signature part. 'Mmm...now that's interesting. I'll take a photo of it and get Chewy to find out who the artist is, was, or is supposed to be.'

The response came back quickly from Chewy. Nic read the text and then looked at Rose. 'It might be a good fake, with a good fake signature.'

Rose picked up the painting. 'So, who is the artist?'

Nic stood up and pushed Dog off his lap. 'Let's say it shouldn't be sitting in a box in the back of a car, and I think I'd better find out why... I've got to make some calls.' He then moved down the stairs with the painting under his arm, and not long after, his Mustang drove away.

Dog had bounded after him.

Rose called out. 'Damn you, Nic, bring it back. The cat, not the painting.'

CHAPTER 15

A couple of days later, the Art Show was looming ever closer. They hadn't heard from Nic, so they decided to meet up with Rose's parents to get an insight into whatever and whoever was expected at the event. They stood outside Rose's parent's property, waiting to be let in at the front gate.

Sandy nodded towards the balcony. 'I can't believe it's been over two years since Nic turned up, riding his pony and called out Rose-rapunzel, Rose-rapunzel let down your hair.'

'It was his Ford Mustang. He was driving in it, not riding it, and besides, I had shorter hair back then, so there was no climbing up the castle wall to rescue me.'

Meantime, the housekeeper had come to the gate and opened it for them to enter the sprawling front garden. Rose nodded. 'Thank you, Mrs Croud.'

Sandy whispered to Rose. 'Why don't you have a key to your parent's place? You had the combination to the gate, too.'

'I returned the key and asked Mrs Croud to change the numbers. There are too many memories here. I've moved on and out. I certainly don't feel I needed to keep being a pigeon that comes home to roost.'

Rose's mother, Jana, was now at the front door and stepped out to greet them. 'Rosemary, your Father is in another of his foul moods, so don't expect anything civil from him until he's settled down.'

Sandy looked at her. 'What's happened?'

'He finished his last bottle of thirty-five-year-old Laphroaig last night.'

Sandy continued. 'So why is that a bad thing? He could buy another.'

Rose sighed. 'He wasted it drinking with Michael, didn't he?'

Jana nodded. 'Yes. That man of yours should remember that it is Father's favourite tipple and shouldn't be guzzled like lemonade.'

Rose shook her head. 'Please, Mother, don't use those four words together; they are ugly and un-truthful. Michael was never a man of mine, he's lucky he ever made it to an adult. I'm surprised Father still lets him in the house.'

'Well, he is our Accountant, and his lovely daughters are a delight when they come over from next door.'

Sandy smiled. 'So, they found a new place to call home and settled in next door?'

'Oh no, that's where the children go after school. I don't think Dimond has found a new place yet.'

Sandy looked at her. 'Dimond doesn't work, so why does she put the children into after-school care?'

Rose looked at her. 'Don't go there, Sandy.'

Meantime, Zachariah overheard the commotion and stepped out of his office. 'Rosemary, he will always be the right man for you. One day, you will realise that and stop flouncing around with that no-good mystery man, Nic Thorn. When will he put a ring on your finger?'

'Father, please don't compare what I have with Nic to what I never had with Michael.' Sandy interjected as she could sense the conversation was getting tense. 'Zachariah, can you tell us the latest with the Art Show?'

Jana let them into the house, and Rose noticed the Brett Whitely painting had been moved from the office. 'So Father, will your fake painting be the pride of place at the show?'

Her father nodded. 'Of course, Rosemary, it is one of the best reproductions available, and I certainly do not need you to remind me of it. Mother told me you had discovered a box of art. Do you want to put any of those into the show?'

'Yes, if we can. We have a couple that might do the trick, but that's the thing, Father, we'll only have them on display if you declare that they are fakes, not for sale.'

'I can do that. Anything else, Rosemary?'

'Well, yes. I assume you have investigated the provenance of the art on display?' Her Father looked at her sternly. 'Just what are you implying?'

'The provenance, Father. The record of who owned them and when. The detailed information about who bought and sold the artwork.' Rose could sense her emotions rising.

'Yes, I know what that is, young lady. What is your concern with the art pieces?'

'Father, I'm a little worried about this thing you're getting mixed up in. Your name is the only one on the lease agreement and....'

Jana finally interrupted them and broke the tension. 'Stop it, Rosemary. Your Father knows what he is doing, and you must trust him.'

'It's just that....' Sandy put her hand on Rose's arm, trying to alleviate the situation. 'Come on, Rose, we've got other things to do today.'

Zachariah looked at Rose. 'You know you really should give him another chance.'

'Who?'

Jana interrupted them again. 'Michael, he's such a lovely man. He does dote after Dimond and their children.'

'He's supposed to. That's one job he has to do well, and he's married and everything.'

'Well, that's something that can be forgiven in due course. Forgive and forget.'

Rose looked at her Mother. 'What's that supposed to mean? Since *my* wedding day, *my* motto is to rue and regret.'

Her Mother looked at her. 'It's been over ten years, Rosemary. You should be well and truly over it by now and found someone else, and it's about time you got yourself a real job.'

Sandy shook her head in dismay. 'I think we've got something else to do. Nic wants us to help him investigate the thing.' Rose nodded, but her Father continued anyway. 'You know, Rosemary, a man like Nic Thorn should not be allowed to command your time as he does. We don't like it, and it certainly must be scaring off any suitable suitors.'

'We don't need any suitors to woo us, Father. We can both woo anyone we want to; when we want to woo and how we want to woo is not up to you. Besides, we had a real job, our couture outlet, but the government closed it down when they built the new road.'

Zachariah shook his head this time. 'We offered to set you up in one of our commercial properties, but you and Sandy declined.'

Rose looked at him. 'And have you as our landlord? That wouldn't have worked.'

Jana clasped her hands together. 'Please stop bickering, you two. How about a nice cup of tea? Mrs Croud, please put the kettle on.'

Rose took a deep breath. 'Make mine a chai latte, please.'

Sandy laughed. 'Mine too.'

Jana looked over at them. 'Since when have you started drinking that silly drink? It's not even real coffee.'

Rose rolled her eyes. 'It's a tea-based drink. Besides, it's good for your skin.'

'Don't forget about the weight loss benefits too, Rose.'

'Thanks, Sandy, but all the running around we do with Nic keeps me trim enough, and speaking of Nic, Father, how much do you know about the crowd putting this art thing together?'

'Why is it any interest of yours, young lady?'

'Well, that's part of what Sandy and I do. We find out about stuff, look into stuff, and, most of the time, solve stuff without hurting people.

Zachariah looked at her. 'Yes, Michael told me.'

'Oh, what else has Michael told you about what we get up to with Nic and his investigations?'

'Nothing much, other than you seem to spend a lot of time travelling together, and you don't have jobs, yet manage to keep food on the table and the bills paid. You could come back and live with us, Rosemary, and stop wasting your life with futile and frivolous pursuits.'

Rose shook her head in dismay. 'I live with Sandy. We've just come back from Dubai looking into a diamond scam, We've also brought down an international wine scammer and reptile smuggler in Perth. Besides that, it's what we do now. We are scam busters. It's all legal, well respected and gives us both a purpose.'

Jana looked at her. 'So is Accounting, Rosemary. You could always work with Michael. He would have you back in a heartbeat.' This time, Sandy and Rose both shook their heads.

Jana finished her coffee and held her cup, commanding the housekeeper to collect it. 'Mrs Croud, please tell Mr Croud to prepare the Bentley, as Mr Palmer and I have a meeting at a Bowen Hills warehouse.' The conversation lulled whilst Mrs Croud collected the cups and saucers, placed them into the dishwasher and moved towards the back door. Sandy took that as a prompt. 'Rose and I are leaving now and will see ourselves out.'

Rose and Sandy followed Mrs Croud into the backyard, where the staff were by the Bentley waiting for further directions from Rose's parents. Rose walked up to them. 'Hello, John, and I'm sorry, Julia if you overheard all of that. I still find my parents are a little hard to take at times.'

Mr Croud stopped cleaning the car window. 'Don't worry about it, Rose. We've both come to terms with them, and we've been here for almost twenty years. It might be time to move on anyway.'

'Will you be OK?'

'Yes, our son and his wife have been running a caravan park in the Daintree, and it's about time we went up there and worked with them. So many grey nomads are around, and the job is getting too big for him. They've got the new twins, Daisy and Maisie, so they need a hand with a few things.'

'That sounds great. I'm happy for you. Have you told Jana and Zachariah as yet?' Julia shook her head. 'Well, that's the thing. We originally had a ten-year contract with bi-annual options to extend, and somehow, they've forgotten about it. We might buy a Camper Van one day and not come back.'

'Let me know when, and we'll put some calls out. Nic has contacts in the motor industry.'

John and Julia looked at each other. 'How about this weekend? We have about a hundred thousand to put towards it.'

Rose looked at them. 'Is that your life savings? Don't put it all into a Winnebago.'

'No, but thanks for asking. We've been lucky over the years. We have quite a bit of savings and have been putting money into our superannuation. We have managed to keep our living expenses low living here and working for your parents.'

They hugged and overheard Zachariah calling out: 'Mr. Croud, please meet us around the front in about five minutes. We will be driving to a warehouse at Bowen Hills.'

Sandy nodded. 'Hey, we've been to the Bowen Hills warehouse precinct a few times. What's the address?'

'It's 11 Exhibition Street, just near the Ekka Showgrounds. I believe they are meeting with a Mr Creosote.'

Rose looked at him. 'Are you sure that's his name? It sounds awfully familiar.'

'Yes, they received a text this morning from the warehouse management. This Mr Creosote has a big reputation, apparently.'

Rose smiled again. 'I bet that's not the only big thing about him either. Anyway, we'll meet you there.'

'You can both ride with us in the Bentley.'

'No thanks, we've already called an Uber.' Rose and Sandy hugged them and moved through the expansive backyard towards the rear gate. The Uber was waiting, and the driver nodded that he knew where they needed to go. They waited for the driver to put in earbuds, and Sandy began.

'Nic told me you went surfing. How did that go? Do you miss it?'

'Yes, it's been a while. I spent some time with Uncle G-P but didn't learn much about how he fits into the Nic Thorn world. I called him 'Garry Pants' when we were being tied up by Ivan the T, so maybe we could start calling him Garry instead?'

CHAPTER 16

About fifteen minutes later, they arrived at the warehouse. Rose's parents were not yet there, so Sandy went to the door to read the nameplate: 'Lumberjacks & IMOK.' There was a highlighted button above the 'j', so she pressed it. The door chimed, and Rose recognised the tune.

'I know that song, Sandy. It's from one of the Monty Pythons films.'

'Which one?'

'The Life of Brian, the name Mr Creosote, is a character from one of the other films. I won't be surprised if Nic is part of this.'

'He can't be; surely he would have told us?'

'I don't know. It depends on how much he's discovered about the paintings and whether it's all a scam. I would say he's keeping us out of the loop to protect my Father.'

Rose was about to knock on the large roller door when it started to open and revealed a rather sizeable overweight gentleman on the other side. He was leaning heavily on a walking cane, wearing a tartan kilt, and looked about eighty years old. 'Hello, laddies. My nume is Creosote, Monty Creosote. I am so vurry pleased to make your lovely acquaintances. I um the paladin of the puntings that are sturred here until the uxhibition. I was uxpecting the Palmers, but I don't think you are quite thum.' His accent had a strong Scottish lilt.

Rose smiled. 'Hello, Nic. I know that's you under all that disguise. Father is on his way in the Bentley, and that's probably them now.'

They watched as the majestic car pulled to a stop. It took up two car spaces in the narrow street. The large man acknowledged Rose's comment, then waddled backwards and swept his arm forth. 'Please unter. The paintings are being stored in a lucked cage down the buck of the room.'

The two women led Creosote toward the area, and the overweight man was struggling with the speed of their steps. He stopped for a breath. 'I'm terrubly sorry, laddies; I'm just not fast enough anymure. My leg. I lust it during the war, and stull gives me griff.' He tapped his cane at his shin, which resounded with a wooden 'clunk.'

Sandy grimaced at the sound. 'Wow, did you lose your entire leg?' The man started to move slowly again. 'Yus, but it's merely a flesh wound.'

Meantime, Zachariah and Jana entered the warehouse and were hurrying to catch up. 'Stop, Creosote, stop. I am the client here. You should not be dealing with those two. You take direction from me and only me.' Rose and Sandy ignored the command, arrived at the storage unit, and waited for the others as it was locked. Creosote extracted a key for the padlock to open the gate. 'The puntings have been catalogued, categorised, cleaned, and coddled. We are ready for delivery on Thursday afternoon. I have my crew lucked in and trucks on stund-by. Have I mussed anything, Mr Palmer?'

'I don't think so, Creosote. I want to see the inventory schedules, and Jana will tell you how you will set up the exhibition. The weather looks like it will be favourable, so we are going with Plan A. The canvas gazebos will contain the art pieces on display outside in the grassed area, along with the remainder of the art on display inside the entry hall.'

The portly man nodded, handed over a folder containing the details of the paintings, and Zachariah flicked through it. 'Seems like everything is in order here, Creosote. I'll be taking this folder with me. You will need to take a copy.'

'Sure and thunk you. I already huve a cuppy Mr Palmer. I'll let my team know that we huve the final go ahud.'

Zachariah dismissed the comment and looked at Rose. 'Right then. Jana and I have something important to tell you, Rosemary. We discussed on the way over here that you can take control of the Art Show from now on. Make sure it all arrives in time, that sort of thing. Please do not disappoint us.'

Rose stared back, then whispered to Sandy. 'Just another decision made without asking me.' Jana overheard. 'What's that, Rose?'

'Nothing Mother. Sandy and I are between engagements now. We will take on Father's little art project on one condition.'

Zachariah shook his head. 'I will not be paying you.'

'No, that's not it. As we will be representing Nic Thorn and Associates, we want to be a part of the security team and have full access to the security protocols.'

Zachariah laughed. 'There is no security team, Rosemary. The Art exhibition is being put on by my colleagues, and I can personally vouch for all of them. It does not require any scrutiny.'

Jana put her hand on Zachariah's arm. 'Let Rosemary have her little fling with it. It might prompt her into finding some real work.'

Sandy looked over to Rose and was surprised at how well she had taken that last comment, but Creosote then broke any tension as he started hiccupping rather loudly, almost too loud. It was as if he would gorge his lunch but regain his composure. 'I'm terribly surry, it's the haggis I had this morning. It's not behuving itself.'

Zachariah again ignored the Scotsman and again looked at Rose. 'Mother and I are leaving now. We will see you Friday morning at the Maritime Museum. You will have completed the art installation before we arrive and will not deviate from our placement of the pieces. The viewing starts at eleven a.m.'

Sandy held down Rose's arm, believing she was about to mock-salute her Father as they watched them leave. Rose sighed. 'At least they think I'm capable of doing something.'

Creosote had moved over to a closed door at the back of the warehouse and knocked on it. 'You can cume through now, Nic Thurn.'

Rose smiled, waited for the answer, and was surprised when Nic responded from the other side. 'Have they gone yet?'

They realised Nic and the Scotsman had conned them: 'If Creosote is not Nic, could it be Garry under all the latex?' The man looked at them, smiled, and then led them to another area where several portrait-sized wooded boxes were stacked.

Sandy looked them over. 'What are these for?'

'We're testing them to determine how the scam might work.' The man's Scottish accent had slipped, so he quickly repeated his last sentence. '*We're tushting thum to see how the scum mught wurk,*' but this time, it came out like someone trying to imitate Sean Connery's famous brogue.

Rose looked at him, then patted the man's rubbery face. 'Hi, Nic. It's a good trick with the voice projection from the other side of the closed door. Was it a mobile phone on loudspeaker?'

The rubber-faced man coughed. 'Damn it, Rose. How did you know?'

'Well, you can put on a large rubber suit, add the tartan kilt, change your face with a latex mask, and talk with a dodgy Scottish accent, but you can't hide your big brown dreamy chocolate eyes.'

Nic responded. 'Next time, I'll remember to use coloured contact lenses.' He then twirled around, the kilt swirled, and the women gasped. Rose feverishly waved her hand at her face. 'Don't do that, Nic, it's unwise, and here's a tip for the future: shave your legs when wearing a skirt, even if it's a Scottish one...'

Nic moved into the metal cage for privacy, opened a carry bag and started to step out of the kilt. He removed the latex mask and body padding, then stepped back into the main area five minutes later dressed in jeans and a button-down shirt.

Sandy looked at him. 'Since when does Superman use a closet? I always thought it was a phone booth.'

Nic was holding a folded page of paper and laid it on a nearby table. It was a hand-drawn map of the Maritime Museum site, and then he took the classic 'Superman' pose with hands on hips. 'I can't fight the future anymore, Lois, everyone uses mobile phones.'

He resigned his hero pose and continued: 'I've had my guys mock up the site's plans.' The print-out showed the location of the Brisbane River to the museum site and the main workshop building.

Nic pointed to five small rectangles in a semi-circle on the grassed area adjacent to the river. 'The guys are setting up the tents that house the art pieces for sale, and any fake paintings will be displayed in the entrance hall. They'll be clearly labelled.' Sandy nodded. 'This all appears to be well organised but how did you get Rose's Father to agree to have you look after the art here at Bowen Hills? This looks like a lumber warehouse, not an art shed.' Rose smiled. 'Any processed timber is called 'lumber' in North America, and here in Australia, we just call it all timber.' Rose broke into a chorus from the Monty Python Lumberjack song and Nic joined her. Sandy interjected. 'Stop singing, you're scaring the bats.'

They moved through the door, and Nic led them into the rear of his warehouse as it was in the same commercial complex. Rose realised where they were. 'I still don't get why Father let you guard all of his art.'

Nic smiled. 'It all comes down to the cost. I had one of my guys follow your Father around for a couple of weeks and hinted to him that he knew where some warehouse storage space was available.'

'So?'

'He told him it was free of charge.'

The trio moved inside and met up with Seiko and Dee-Dee, working on some empty wooden crates. 'We've been looking at the different ways the purchaser can get scammed out of getting their piece of art. One of them is the old switcheroo, by taking the real painting 'out the back' to box it up, then replacing it with a fake, then another is that the painting is a fake, to begin with. There's always the 'send me the money, and I'll post it to you' scam, too.'

Rose nodded. 'That sounds all pretty simple, but what's the take on this one?'

'We're not sure yet. Each painting is sold in a wooden crate specially made for the portrait. We thought about opening one to see if that was how they were doing the scam, but it may have raised suspicion, so we have matched the invoices against the QR codes.'

Rose nodded again. 'Did the code scan confirm the provenance?'

'Yes. It's very well organised and appears genuine. There's even a link back to the artist. It seemed a little over the top as the most expensive painting here is worth about twenty thousand. Most of them are around five thousand.'

Rose shook her head. 'And then there are the fakes on display in the entry hall.'

Nic nodded. 'I know. According to the site plan, each tent will house five paintings. They're attached to the wooden support studs inside the tents and then hung with small metal rings attached to the back of the frame. They have five tents in different styles, including portraits, landscapes, watercolours, water scenes and buildings. The prints in the entry hall show anything left over. At this stage, everything looks legitimate.'

Sandy added the total. 'That's about thirty all up. Roughly a hundred thousand dollars' worth.'

Nic continued: 'I think there's more than that as they might introduce new stock as each painting is sold. That could be where the scam is, but we haven't seen any other artwork. They might even throw in a couple of sculptures if there's room, and I expect they want to sell them all. We've done some background checks, and the exhibition process started about twelve months ago. That was around when the company name 'It Keeps Changing' was registered, but we could not find any other names linked to the project. Zachariah will take the fall alone if it all goes south.'

'Father will talk his way out of it and blame everyone else. It's what he does.'

Nic smiled at Rose's comment. 'Anyhow, we need to find out who the rest of the geezers are and have put a portfolio together with what little we know. We've called them Bashful, Dopey, Happy, Sleepy, and others.

'Snow White?'

'No, I think it's another ..um....affliction ....Coughy? Sleazy? Snoopy?'

Sandy shook her head. 'I think it's Droopy, as you missed a bit of the latex, and it's stuck to your nose.'

Nic tweaked his nose, but there was nothing there. 'Anyway, we don't have much to work on until Thursday when the pre-show begins. Let's finish up here and go to lunch. Anyone up for black pudding?'

They were going to the door at the back of the warehouse when Rose picked up the walking cane. 'How did you make the wooden clunk sound when you tapped your leg?'

'Tap it on the ground, then against your leg..' Rose followed the prompt, and the cane made the same sound. 'Clever cane, but what's the trick?'

Nic took it back from her, slid up a small cover plate near the crook and pulled out a computer chip. 'It's an interchangeable sound bite. You can make it woof, meow and moo or record your voice and play it back. The switch is the rubber stopper. It's just another product thing that Chewy has been working on. It's a great gift the kids can get for their Grandpa. That's what we do: find stuff, fake stuff, and make stuff up.'

Rose smiled. 'I know someone I'd love to give one to. Can I get it to say, 'Get Stuffed?'

CHAPTER 17

It was Thursday, around nine in the morning, when Rose and Sandy arrived at the Maritime Museum to rehearse the Art Show and Shine. They went through the entrance hall and noticed the 'fake' prints were already hung on the walls. Zachariah's 'painting' and two from Rose's collection were labelled: 'Not for Sale – viewing only'.

Two men stared at the art pieces, so they wandered over to them. 'Hi, I'm Rose Palmer. These are part of my Father's collection.' The older man was startled by the statement and then looked at her. 'This is a fake young lady. Why is it on display?' Rose ignored the comment. 'So why are you both here so early? The show is not until Saturday.'

The younger man responded. 'We're checking it all before we finally commit to anything. I'm Blake Beasley, and this is my Father, Chris. It's part of our collection that will be set up outside and....' The older man glared at his son. 'Quiet, Blake. Now let's go.'

Sandy watched them leave. 'I think we've just met Mr Bashful and Mr Happy.'

Rose and Sandy went up to the painting they'd made available for the show. 'I'm glad Nic let us put this one in. It's a good fake; even the signature looks legit.'

Rose and Sandy then moved through the hall, stepped outside, and traversed the two gangways via 'H.M.A.S Diamantina'.

The boat had been in the Graving Dock since the 1980s after decommissioning. There were also several other decommissioned boats on-site for hands-on inspection, including 'Ella's Pink Lady', the boat that was sailed solo around the world by sixteen-year-old Jessica Watson in 2009.

The exhibition was set up in the large, grassed site on the other side of the work shed, whilst the separate section of the museum workshop housed the fake prints. Rose nodded towards a small stage where Nic, Carly and Crusoe set up their equipment. Nic had agreed he would lay low during the exhibition, after all, he was only with the band.

They duly ignored them and headed to the other end of the promenade to take in the view of the Brisbane River. It was currently low tide, and they could see glimpses of the muddied brown beach at the bottom of the river wall.

'It's high tide around two o'clock today and tomorrow, but the river height won't get up as high as the wall, so the paintings won't get wet.'

'Good to know. I hoped you weren't planning to jump into the river if dealing with your Father gets too much.' Rose smiled. 'Not until high tide, it'll be about three metres deep. Otherwise, I'll get a sore head.'

They turned around and approached the tents where the art pieces were being installed. Most paintings were hung but didn't have prices at this stage. A young man was struggling with the weight of one of the larger pieces. It was of a Hawaiian Sunset, so Rose lent him a hand. 'This is a nice piece.'

He nodded thanks for her assistance and softly patted the picture frame. 'Yep, and it's the most expensive one here. I reckon y'all should get about thirty thousand.'

They aligned the wires, hooked them into the little rings at the back of the frames and admired their handy work. The man moved on to the next piece, so Rose continued to help with linking, hooking, and hanging.

When the five pieces were turned, he gave her a 'shaka sign' and started to move on to the next tent, but Sandy stopped him. 'So when do the prices get added?'

The man continued. 'Not 'til Sat'day. Today and t'morrow are the Show and Shine days. They will be 'price spies' moving around the show telling ya from feedback what each piece might be worth.'

Sandy continued. 'But what about tonight? Surely they won't be left outside for two days?'

'No, they'll take them down when your event closes at four and carry them to the work shed for overnight storage. They're put back into the wooden crates, then re-hung in the morning. Hopefully, they get an offer on some paintings before the sale day, otherwise, y'all get sore arms.'

The young man again gave the 'shaka sign' and moved away. Rose and Sandy watched him for a while, then moved to the stage area where the band were setting up for their rehearsal. Nic continued to ignore them so Sandy looked around for a seat. 'So what's that thumb and pinkie thing?'

Rose smiled. 'It's from Hawaii. I went surfing there once. It means 'hang loose', ' be cool', 'thanks', or something like that.

Nic was standing up plucking away at a cello, Crusoe was tuning his guitar, Sticks Out was tapping a little paradiddle on his snare, and Carly was going through her pre-vocal routine. Rose and Sandy finally found a seat in bean bags and waited for the rehearsal to begin.

'Check one, two.' Carly tapped the microphone, looked over at Crusoe, who usually attends to the band's sound desk, and he nodded. 'It's on presets, Carly, so we won't be able to change anything.'

Carly continued her routine. 'OK. Ladies and gentlemen, thank you for listening. We're the...um.' Carly looked over to Sticks Out. 'The Pining Parrots' and we'll be here on Saturday for the main event.'

Rose whispered to Sandy. 'That's another quote from a Monty Python skit. I didn't realise Nic had so much influence over these guys.'

Sandy shook her head. 'I think it's Sticks Out. Every time I've been to their place recently, he's been watching the Python film re-runs. He wept for a week when Terry Jones died.'

Nic picked up a bow and began with a legato, and the deep resonance echoed solemnly through the speakers. Carly moved up to the microphone and softly began singing the opening verse of 'Bridge over Troubled Water.' The museum crowd stopped to listen, and when the song finished, even the people walking across the Goodwill Bridge clapped loudly. They moved on to the next song, a jazzy version of 'Bright Eyes' from the 1978 film Watership Down. The second song finished, Carly stepped back to drink water, and Sticks Out moved towards his microphone. 'OK, all you hipsters out there...Why did we start with those two songs?'

The young man Rose and Sandy had been helping before yelled back to him. 'Both are sung by the great man, Art Garfunkel. Good choice, y'all.'

Sticks Out tapped his drumsticks together. 'You're correct. Give that man a painting.'

The band played a few more songs, then started to pack up the equipment, and the young man approached Sticks Out. 'Thanks for the show, y'all. It's going to do well on Saturday. I hope we can get a higher price for our work.'

Sticks nodded. 'Oh, we hope so too. Have you got some of your paintings for sale?' He stammered with his response. 'Err...I'm not sure yet. I have to go.' and he hurried off.

Rose and Sandy stood up and returned to the tents, hoping to learn more details from anyone involved in the show. They were unsuccessful, and at four o'clock, after deciding they'd had enough, they went to Nic's apartment to wait for him. It was around a two-minute walk away.

Nic was already there with an early meal on the table, his laptop open and fingers poised in readiness. 'Well, did you find the rest of the geezers then?'

Rose nodded. 'We met a guy called Blake Beasley and his father, Chris. They hinted that they have some skin in the game so that we can mark off Happy and Bashful.'

Nic entered the names. 'Yep, Blake and Chris Beasley operate an Art Gallery in Melbourne.' He scrolled through their website. 'They have quite a collection for sale. It looks like the most recent auction was a bit of a fizzer, though, as nobody turned up.'

Sandy looked at him. 'Why?'

'Well, my arty craft handy Sandy, their gallery is in the suburb of Jolimont, which puts it near the Melbourne Cricket Ground. They chose the wrong day.'

'What, everyone caught a typical wet, cold, dry and hot day in Melbourne and stayed away?' Nic smiled. 'Not exactly. The Aussie Rules Football finals were on, so the trams weren't running, and no one could get there unless they walked. If they drove, all the streets would have been blocked off.'

'They didn't work that out well then, did they?'

'Probably not, but I enjoyed the game though.'

Rose shook her head. 'So now you tell us you know someone that knows someone that gets you free tickets?' Nic continued. 'Something like that, but not exactly. My sister is married to a football umpire and getting free tickets is about the only benefit of getting yelled at for being wrong all the time. Anyway, did you find anything else out?'

Rose nodded. 'We helped some young guy hang some of the pieces. I saw that hooks were attached to the frames and not onto the back of the paintings, so that may be something. They have made the crates much larger than they should be. I read on the terms and conditions of the sale that the wooden crates are an additional non-negotiable expense for protecting the piece. It might not mean anything, but nothing only means something until it means something.'

Nic smiled. 'Wow. That's real gobble-de-gook, well done.' Rose looked at him. 'So what's next then, my nefariously nasty Nic?'

'We take a late night visit to the museum work shed and check out the crates.'

'It's an electronic keyless panel lock. How will you get the combination? You're not part of the security team.' Nic smiled. 'Nope, but you guys are. Fancy a late-night stroll?' Rose shook her head. 'We haven't been given the combination either. Father thought it wasn't necessary.' Nic nodded. 'I guess I'll play it by ear then. Head home and I'll see you both back here about one o'clock.'

CHAPTER 18

It was two o'clock in the morning when the trio approached the Brisbane River. There was no moon and accordingly, very dark. Rose and Sandy wondered where they were headed as they padded over the paved South Bank pathway. Nic led them in the opposite direction to the Maritime Museum. They were dressed in full-body neoprene wetsuits.

Rose stopped walking when she realised they were almost at the riverbank. 'Damn you, Nic. I hate getting wet.'

'I thought you used to be a champion surfer?'

'I was, but that was long ago in a far-off galaxy.'

'Wow, you must be nervous quoting from Star Wars.'

'Yes, and I'm dressed in black like Darth Vader, so behave yourself.' Rose held her hand and curled her fingers, imitating the space villain's action. 'You are not my son, but you will stop and tell us what we are doing.'

Nic laughed. 'I'll give you that one, *Dad*....We are going via the river to avoid the entrance hall, then wading through the water and scaling the ladder at the wall by the museum. Oh, and breaking into the work shed at two o'clock in the morning.' Rose nodded. 'Right then, thanks. Let's move.'

The water was cold, but only waist deep as they walked towards the ladder.

It was about a hundred metres through the water, but the process was slower than expected, and the soft river sand wasn't helping either. After about half an hour, they reached the wall, and Nic looked up. 'Good, there are fewer rungs than I thought, and that's the good news.'

Rose shivered in the cold water waist-deep as they watched him climb the ladder. 'So what's the bad news?'

Nic reached the top rung and waited for them. 'Sometimes it's just news, Rose, and as they say, any publicity is good.'

Rose and Sandy climbed the ladder and sat on the grass, pulling at their neoprene suits, bathed in the darkness of the moonless night. Sandy looked over to Rose and Nic. 'I suppose this is when Nic tells us how he will bypass the keyless security lock.'

'Not yet, my wily wet-suited waders. First, you must get across the grass, avoid the spotlights and cameras, and ignore the shivering cold without being seen by late-night revellers. Easy.'

Sandy slowly stood up and promptly sat down again. 'I can't feel my feet; maybe they've gone to sleep already. It's too late for my feet to be out unless I'm dancing.'

Rose began rubbing them. 'Yes, they're cold or frozen, or maybe my hands are frozen, as I can't feel her feet either.'

Nic started rubbing them, too. 'It could be that you're wearing gloves.'

Rose stood up and surveyed the scene. 'Err, Nic, why are the lights on inside the work shed? And surely they have cameras on around here at night? I noted where they were earlier, and they rotate through a hundred-and-eighty-degree axis.'

Nic stopped massaging Sandy's feet. 'Why should all that be a problem? They say the light will guide your way, or in this case, it could be they leave the lights on just in case someone wants to break in during the middle of the night.'

Rose looked at him. 'That still doesn't make sense.'

Nic smiled. 'OK then, would you believe it is to ensure the cockroaches don't feast on the still-life art? Or it could be that it's just part of the security protocols to keep the lights on. The cameras are another issue, but Chewy has taken care of that. Let's say that if one can hack into the Wi-Fi that operates the cameras, one can momentarily stop them. He is the one, but in this case, not the Obi-Wan, but the Chewy one.'

Sandy went to stand up again, but the cramp in both calves prevented her from moving further, and she rolled into a foetal position, holding her legs. 'You'll have to go on without me. I can't move.

Now I know how a seal feels after spending all day splashing around in the cold ocean, looking for food. If anything happens, I'll roll into the river and float out to sea. Arf, arf.'

Nic removed Sandy's gloves and blew air into her hands. 'OK, wait here. Rose and I will do this alone, but together. Are you ready, Rose?'

Nic stood and helped Rose up. 'On three, we go... Three,' and they slunk across the grassed area towards the storage shed. Rose kept up with him during the twenty-metre trek, and when they flattened themselves against the corrugated iron of the building, she caught her breath and then whispered.

'Since when do we go on three? It's supposed to be one, two, and then three.'

'Oops, I panicked, but now we are here, we must get in.'

Nic went to pull at the zip on his wetsuit, but it appeared stuck. 'Do you mind? It's an old suit. I might have washed it too often, and it's shrunk.'

Rose shook her head. 'Or maybe you've eaten too many party pies and are a little more... well-rounded.' Rose turned to face him and gave the zipper a pull. It quickly opened to Nic's waist to reveal his well-toned chest.

'You can stop staring now, Rose.' Nic reached inside the wetsuit to pull out an iPhone 'mini'. 'And this is my lock picker.'

'It's a phone, Nic.'

'I know, how good is that?' He selected the microphone/record app and pushed play. The tune played back. *'Doot, Doot, Doot, Doot, Doot, Doot, Doot, Doot.'*

Each tone is slightly different to the next.

Rose looked at him. 'You recorded the eight-digit PIN.'

'Yep, I told you I'd play it by ear. Besides, I didn't want to smash the door open.' Nic pushed the appropriate buttons, but the door didn't open, so he tried the keypad again. The light fluttered green, then back to red.

'Well, that's not supposed to happen.'

Rose looked at him. 'Can I have a try?'

Nic nodded and waved his hand at the pad. 'Be my guest.'

Rose pressed the buttons, and the light turned green. 'Maybe I've got magic fingers, or I had asked my Father what the combination was.....Have a guess which one.'

Nic smiled, then pressed a button on his phone, and an audible countdown commenced: *'Two hundred and forty....Two hundred and thirty-nine....'*

Rose hesitated. 'Won't they notice someone's accessed the door in the middle of the night?'

'Maybe if the Security Base gets suspicious, but Chewy will take care of that too. He'll call them in a few minutes and explain that *it was 'us' and we are doing a maintenance check on the data lines.* He'll apologise and reset it so there'll be no entry and exit record. By the way, we have about four minutes for the search.'

Two hundred and Twenty...

'That still doesn't make sense. Surely it couldn't be that easy?'

Two hundred and ten...

'It's nearly three o'clock in the morning. The night shift Security Team is usually one guy who struggles to keep awake without his Red Bull; besides that, he won't need to report it in the morning as there won't be any evidence that anything happened.'

One hundred and eighty...

Rose and Nic moved inside the packing room, realised the site location, and sorted the paintings. A site map was also on the wall above the crates. Rose located the Hawaiian seascape, so she picked up the crate and placed it on a nearby table.

'I assume the QR code on the crate matches the one on the painting to maintain the provenance.' Rose slid open the balsa wood lid and partially removed the painting to prove her point. 'There's a QR code on the top of each corner. I hadn't noticed that before, and see here, the QR label is not across both painting and frame.'

One hundred and thirty....

Nic made his way through another stack and noticed a broken crate on the floor, so he picked it up for a closer inspection. The four-sided crate had two groves for the wooden inserts. It was double-sided and separated by another piece of balsa wood in the middle.

The lids slid together to close off on both sides but in opposite directions. The crate had access from both sides, and there was a hinge along the bottom part of the frame, but only on one side. Nic tested the hinge, and it moved freely.

'This is quite a set-up to carry the art, and I suspect these paintings could be stored in a much thinner crate.' He took some photos with his phone.

Fifty five...fifty four...

They looked around a little longer.

'We've seen enough. Sandy must be frozen by now.'

Thirty five....thirty four...

Nic and Rose were finally about to leave when they heard a scraping noise on the other side of the door.

Fifteen...fourteen...

Rose stopped. 'I think we have been sprung, and what happens if we don't get out in time?'

Nic put his forefinger to his lips so they kept still and listened for more sounds. 'It could just be river rats. They grow pretty big around these parts.'

Three... two...one....

Rose looked over to Nic, but his expression hadn't changed. No panic: everything is under control, and business as usual.

'Hey Nic and Rose, are you finished in there yet?'

Nic looked at Rose, 'Oh my, the big river rat knows our names.'

'It's me, Sandy.'

'Oh no, Rose, there's a big rat out there, and it wants to introduce itself to us.'

Rose shook her head. 'We're coming out, Sandy. What's up?'

They stepped outside of the work shed, and Nic secured the door.

'Um...I was lying in the darkness contemplating myself and the universe when I saw a flotilla of blue lights approaching me.'

Nic looked at her. 'What a real UFO! The truth is out there, you know.'

'Nope, you dope who wants to elope with Dana and Fox. They're on the river and looked like Police boats.'

Nic tapped at his ear. *'Seiko. Police presence. North Quay.'*

He waited momentarily for a response. 'OK. Fine. See you tomorrow. Over.' Nic looked at Sandy. 'They've found a submerged car not far from here. We'd better get moving anyway, but if we get caught, we can tell them we're part of the security team guarding the paintings.'

Rose whispered. 'It's three o'clock in the morning.'

'Maybe we're the night shift?'

Rose shook her head. 'Err... there is another issue. We're dressed in wetsuits.'

'Oh yeah, there is that.'

The group avoided the river and slunk their way back to Nic's place via the main entrance hall, and when they exited the building, Rose looked back into the venue to notice all the cameras were pointing up towards the ceiling. *Well done, Chewy.*

In the meantime, Sandy looked for footprint evidence on the tiled floor. 'What if they see our footprints?'

'We'll tell them Aquaman wanted a sneak peek at the watercolours. Atlantis always needs more art as the canvas keeps getting soggy.'

About forty minutes later, they had all showered and were getting warmer. 'It's nearly four in the morning, guys; what do you want to do now?'

Rose was sitting at the dining room table, and Sandy was lying on the sofa. 'Are we having a rest now? It's too late, as we've lost Sandy already.'

Nic smiled. 'OK, let's have a kip for a couple of hours. We don't have to return to the exhibition until at least ten today. The bed in the second bedroom is already made up and.....' Rose stood up and headed to her room.

'What about the troll that lives under your bed? Does it tend to go wandering?'

'Nope.'

Rose then returned with a blanket for Sandy. 'I've set the alarm for nine-thirty. If I'm not up, wake me up before you go. I don't plan on going solo.'

Nic laughed. 'I'll wham the door just in case.'

Just before nine-thirty, Rose woke to the aroma of ground coffee, then heard Sandy calling out from the kitchen. 'Help. It won't stop.' Rose straightened the quilt, karate-chopped the pillows and left the bedroom.

'I'm coming, Sandy. Where's Nic?'

'I think he's showering. I wasn't ....I'm not going in there...the ugly troll....'

Rose watched as a puff of powdered coffee cloud billowed from the grinder. 'Wow, that looks serious. I wonder if it's supposed to do that.'

'I've no idea, but at least the splashback is dark brown to hide the mess.' The apartment's front door opened as they scrambled to switch the coffee maker off at the PowerPoint. 'Guys, it's me, and I've got coffee and tofu doughnuts.'

Rose left the kitchen calamity and assisted him with the supplies. Nic noticed the mess in the kitchen, smiled, and moved over to open the sliding balcony doors to let some fresh air into the apartment. 'I hate it when it does that.'

Sandy looked at him. 'So, it wasn't me then?'

'Nope. It's something else Chewy has been working on, evidently with little success. Everyone enjoys morning coffee, so he's worked on a machine that percolates the perfect cup. Don't worry;

the dust bunnies will clean it up once they finish in my bedroom.'

'And yet you left us alone with the troll and the bunnies and ventured off to buy coffee?'

'Yep, you're perfectly safe as long as you don't look them in the eye or feed them after midnight. Besides, I love the smell of burnt coffee grounds in the morning. Let's do breakfast; then we've got more snooping to catch up on. So far, we've tracked down four people involved in the exhibition. Blake and Chris Beasley are from Melbourne, and the mother and son are from Hawaii.'

Nic turned the television on and uploaded photos of the alleged suspects and the broken crate he'd taken in the work shed. 'I've been trying to work out why the crates would be double-sided but couldn't come up with anything. They've made the crates wide enough to take two paintings, but they only carry one. I don't understand what the hinge is needed for yet. I had Chewy look at the QR codes, which all appear legitimate.'

Rose nodded and pointed toward the young American. 'We met that guy yesterday. I helped him hang a Hawaiian sunset picture, and he mentioned it was worth about thirty thousand dollars. Why do you think he's involved?'

'Chewy picked up some chatter on the exhibition's Facebook site about a mother and son recently arriving from Hawaii to off-load some paintings they'd inherited. It could be them, so he's accessing the International Airport Arrivals. Can you try and find some more about them?'

Sandy scanned the QR Code and confirmed for herself. 'There's a link and a mobile phone number too. Shall we ring it?'

Rose nodded. 'You're up, Nic.'

Nic entered the number, put his phone on speaker and placed it face up. It answered immediately with a pre-recorded message:

'*Welcome to the only way to buy art. Forget on-line. Keep it real.*'

Rose sighed and leant away from the phone. 'That's my Father's voice.'

Nic nodded, and they continued to listen to the script:

'*My name is Zachariah Palmer. Join us for the Auction at the Maritime Museum in Brisbane. You'll find us on Facebook.*'

The call ended without being able to leave a message, nor did it name the date or time. Rose crossed her arms. 'No mention of whom he represents, where they can contact him or even a website to validate anything. It's just a little ....'

Nic interrupted her. 'Yep. I don't think there's much else to investigate with that. I'll get Chewy to look at the Facebook site as he might be able to find out who uploaded it, and he'll review blurbs about the buyer's and seller's conditions of the auction. Anyway, we have about half an hour before getting back there. Is there anyone else we should be looking at?'

Rose continued. 'So far, we've tracked down Bashful and Happy. Let's call the young man Dopey and his mother, Mrs White. That leaves only two more, Sleepy and Sneezy.'

Nic smiled. 'So look for someone yawning a lot and another one with bad allergies.'

CHAPTER 19

To maintain the ruse that they weren't working together, Nic delayed his arrival for more than two hours as the band was not due to start playing until 1 p.m. When Nic finally arrived, he noticed Rose conversing deeply with her Father. Nic was amused. It was amicable, and Sandy managed to manoeuvre away over to him and the band.

'Hi, Carly. Have you got the song list together yet? Do you think I can step up and do some sultry singing, too?'

Carly nodded. 'Sure...I think you could sing better than Crusoe anyway...he's having singing lessons, but it still sounds like ...well...at least the dogs can hear him.'

In the meantime, Nic remained in earshot and was busying himself, plugging and unplugging, wrapping microphone leads, and unwrapping guitar leads. He crouched down and gently tapped Sandy's foot.

'What's going on?'

Sandy turned her back on Rose and Zachariah and kept her voice low. 'After our little snooping thing last night, Rose insisted on reporting to her Father that the security protocols needed to be taken more seriously, but he's fine with whatever happens. It's as if he's expecting something, or he could just be oblivious.'

Nic nodded. 'Did you find anything more about Mrs White and Dopey?'

'Well, they're here only for the exhibition. About an hour ago, Carly and I argued about Hawaii, the best island to visit, and fortunately, we were close enough for Dopey and his mother to get involved. They were a little guarded about their itinerary, but we discovered they have more than one painting here for sale. The main one is the Hawaiian piece, and it's recently been valued by an Auction House at ten thousand, not the thirty he said it was worth yesterday. They did mention it's insured for twenty-five thousand dollars.'

'Maybe he was talking it up?'

'He could be. Should we keep an eye on him and her?'

'Sounds like a plan, but keep it casual. They might be a confused cog in all the frosty fraud fog.' Sandy sighed. 'So it's a scam then?'

Nic nodded. 'I'm going to call it a 'yep', and Zachariah could be heading for a fall. We can't find anything more about who is putting this together as they're very good at hiding themselves. It's as if they work in a mine all day with those little lamps on their heads. Hi-Ho, Hi-Ho...it's off to scam we go.'

Sandy and Rose were now watching the paintings being re-installed in the appropriate tents when the serenity was interrupted by the throbbing sounds from a horde of jet skis. Seven Sea-Doos were skimming atop the Brisbane River in a 'V' formation.

The riders zoomed under the Captain Cook Expressway spanning the river, then slowed down as they went under the Goodwill Pedestrian Bridge adjacent to the Museum site. A super-hero was riding each craft, and a giant flag was held between the last two riders:

'Welcome to Brisbane Comic-Con.'

Sandy nodded towards the leader. 'I didn't realise Superman rode those little things. I know Batman has his own sleek black batty speed boat, so why bother with those noisy floaty boaty machines?'

The remainder of the Museum crowd watched as the super-seven, which included an Iron Man, a Robin, a Spiderman, a Wonder Woman, and an Aqua-man, skilfully manoeuvre their way through the river swell.

Rose responded: 'Well, at least most of them have superpowers, but I never understood why Batman had his little nerdy birdy man along for the ride.'

Nic ambled up and whispered. 'I think you mean Robin. He's a cool guy. Everyone needs a wing-man or a wing-woman, and sometimes they don't have any superpowers.'

The art crowd now wandered towards the end of the grassy plateau to gain a better view of the parade, and the jet skis had slowed down sufficiently to reduce their ride to a slow crawl. All the onlookers were cheering.

Rose noticed another aluminium run-about containing another two super-heroes, and another Aqua-man at the helm was operating the outboard whilst another Spiderman was standing aft. 'Hey Nic, since when did superheroes come in plural?'

'Well, there was that documentary recently with all the Spider-men.'

'That was a cartoon, Nic.'

'Yep, but it could have been based like most cartoons are. The Simpsons family are so lifelike.'

The little boat skimmed behind the super-seven and momentarily disappeared out of view, hidden by the river wall at the end of the grassy plateau. Suddenly, Spiderman clambered up over the wall from the river-side area. The masked man ran up to the tent holding the Hawaiian painting, casually unhooked it from the wall space, and then walked backwards to the river wall with the painting in front of him. The Museum group watched the heist, and finally, Rose raised the obvious.

'Err Nic, I believe he's stealing the painting....'

'Probably, but I'm not known for running a hundred metres in under ten seconds. I'm not The

Flash, you know. Let's see if someone else takes control of the situation. After all, where can he go? The river is behind him...it is high tide...and I'm currently with the Band.'

Meantime, Zachariah had made his way over to Rose. 'I think that young man is stealing a painting Rosemary. I have appointed you Security, so what are you doing about it?'

Rose looked at him. 'Well, Father...the river is behind him, and it is high tide...and besides, I'm currently with the Band.'

The 'Spidey' thief moved to the end of the plateau but still had his back to the river and appeared to be waiting for something. Rose then noticed a long, plastic, slender pole wavering behind him, and the rod tapped at the man's back. He'd gathered it with his hand and threaded it through two round loops at the back of the painting. Some of the crowd started to react, but the man kept his focus.

He then let it go, and the painting dropped to whoever was waiting below; then, he looked at the maddening crowd. 'Don't move. Any of you.'

The voice was metallic, sounding like Darth Vader with a head cold. He then bowed and dove backwards into the river behind him.

By now, some of the crowd had decided to pursue him, but by the time they had reached the end of the plateau, the man had clambered onto the back of the motorboat, and the two thieves had made their getaway. The boat quickly gained speed, and a couple of seconds later, they were well across the 450-metre-wide river, almost to the other side. The painting had been secured in what appeared to be a waterproof pouch.

Meanwhile, the 'V' formation of superheroes was further up the river, away from all the excitement in front of the Museum area. Sandy shook her head. 'So much for a bunch of superheroes on jet skis. None of them noticed, and I was looking forward to a super-stylish spectacle.'

Rose and Sandy finally made their hundred-metre dash to the river to join the others, watching all the commotion. All anyone could do was watch as the duo skilfully evaded a couple of passing River Ferries and quickly made it to the bank on the other side. They quickly leapt onto a North Shore riverside platform and decamped towards the University carpark area.

A woman hurried from the painting storage area. 'Someone call the Police. Where's the Security? That man just stole my painting. I knew this would happen. We should have stayed in Hawaii. I want it back.'

Zachariah walked up to her. 'My daughter, Rosemary, is part of the Security Team, but she couldn't stop him. We don't have insurance to cover theft, as we didn't expect anyone to try anything. Are you self-insured?' The woman continued ranting.

'Yes, but that's not the point. I want you to explain to me how you let this happen.'

Rose stepped forward. 'I'm sorry for your loss.' The woman glared at her. Rose continued. 'Actually, that's not the correct expression for losing artwork. I'll endeavour to have it returned to you as soon as possible, and I believe you were here with your son. We haven't seen him around this morning.'

The woman continued glaring. 'Why? Just what are you implying, young lady?'

'Nothing as yet, but he'll need to be interviewed too. We have to eliminate him from being part of the heist.'

Zachariah glared at Rose. 'You will do nothing of the sort; these people are my guests.'

'That's fine, Father. I'll follow the evidence and see where this investigation takes me. Each ferry has onboard twenty-four-hour cameras operating; three were in the general vicinity at the time. I'm sure I'll gain access to the vision once I call the Police.'

The woman was seething. 'Your Father told me you were just the security. I don't think you're with the Police. You would not have access to that information so readily. Just who do you think you are?'

Meanwhile, Nic had moved closer to the group to understand where the conversation was heading. Rose noticed Nic in her peripheral vision and responded. 'Sandy and I are licenced Private Investigators, and the Police tend to appreciate any assistance resolving theft and frauds.'

Nic smiled. *Touché, Rose.*

Rose continued. 'I'll also post on Facebook for anyone who took vision with their cameras. It will likely make headline news tonight, and I'll call my contact on Channel Seven Television.'

The woman quickly stepped backwards with her mouth agape, and then Zachariah assisted her in moving further away. Nic came up to Rose. 'Since when did you two become PIs? There's a study required and everything.'

'It's not that difficult. You can complete it online, and it takes about a month. It's called a Certificate Three in Investigative Services.'

Nic nodded. 'Yep, I know, but I could have claimed your training study as a Business Expense. Tax deduction and all that.'

Sandy shook her head. 'Is that all you can say?'

Nic paused. 'When is the Graduation Ceremony? I've always wanted to see you both dressed in a black Batman cape with a little black flat cap.' Rose shook her head. 'It's called a mortarboard, and a Certificate is not quite a degree. That's a lot more study and costs a lot more money.'

Nic nodded. 'OK then, if you give me the receipts, I'll reimburse you.'

Rose responded. 'Err, we don't keep receipts. That's one thing we've learnt from you. Destroy the paper trail.' Nic continued. 'But didn't you apply online? They would have emailed you the payment receipts?' Rose looked at Sandy and they both shrugged. The group then moved back to the stage area, where Nic re-joined the band to start performing.

About an hour later, Zachariah came barrelling towards Rose and Sandy. 'See what you've done now, and why didn't you stop him? She's leaving and taking five pictures with her. That's five paintings I won't earn the sales commission on. How are you going to make up for that?'

Rose stood up. 'Well, Father, the simple answer is *'I'm not'*. Something is happening here, and you could be left holding the baby.' Jana had now joined her husband and overheard the comment. 'Baby, what baby?' Rose rolled her eyes whilst Jana continued remonstrating.

'What have you done now, Rosemary? At least there'll be a wedding now. Do you at least know who the father is?'

Sandy looked at them. 'It's just an expression of speech, Jana. You know, like, what happens if you assume? It makes an ass....' Rose interrupted her. 'Don't go there, Sandy. We'll get this thing sorted out; besides, we've already had a response from the ferry people, and the vision will be available to us in twenty-four hours.'

Zachariah looked at her. 'Well, I hope you get it sorted out soon, young lady, as it is so embarrassing for me. I left you in charge of the security; this is how you repay me.' Her Father stomped away.

Rose took a deep breath, sat back down, and Sandy looked at her. 'How did you manage to access the vision so quickly?'

'I didn't. Nic did.'

'Damn, I thought being a P.I. gave us superpowers.'

'Nope. Maybe limited powers of persuasion, but that's about it.'

CHAPTER 20

It was nearing 3 p.m., and Rose and Sandy had spent most of the day avoiding Zachariah and Jana and were now helping the Hawaiian vendor load her wares into a removalist van. The woman was giving little away. 'You know, young lady, this has cost me a lot of money.' Rose nodded as they hefted the last paintings into the small van's rear. 'Well, it's just my Father...he's....' Rose decided not to complete her sentence.

The woman looked at her. 'At least I have the opportunity to sell them elsewhere. I've met a man and his son with a boutique Art Gallery in Melbourne, so that's something else I must manage now.'

'I hope that works out for you. It's a big drive, about twenty hours straight. Will you be sharing the driving with your son? I haven't seen him today.' The woman climbed into the van. 'He's at Comic-Con. I'm going to pick him up along the way.'

After watching the van depart, Rose and Sandy checked out the broken crate in the storage area. Fortunately, the crate was still there but had been smashed into smaller pieces and put into a trash bin. Rose pulled out her phone, took more photos, and then located and scanned the QR codes. It read *'Hawaiian Sunset over Waikiki' painted by Aolani Kawaii. Estimated value fifteen thousand dollars.'*

Sandy googled the artist and the painting. It referred back to a recent Auction House in Los Angeles, where the highest bid was refused at twelve thousand. Rose wondered out loud. 'This is the crate, but why is this specific one broken and this specific painting stolen?'

Sandy responded. 'We'll have to ask Spiderman and Aqua-man when we catch up to them. Did Nic get anywhere with the camera vision from the University?'

Rose shook her head. 'Not much. So far, it's shown the thieves running through the Uni grounds and ducking into the Indoor Swimming Pool area. He's checked it out already, but none of the lockers there are big enough to contain a hidden painting. There is also some vision of people leaving the pool area, but Chewy hasn't gone through that yet.'

Sandy smiled. 'OK then. Let's do one round of the site and see if anything else turns up.'

Rose and Sandy were now well in the confines of the work shed and were about to leave the area when two men entered the space. The women stepped back into a darkened room and stood still. The men headed towards a large crate, leaning against a wall. The box was about three metres high and two metres wide. They gathered the wooden box, laid it on the ground and started sliding the panels away. It revealed a large opaque sheet of thick Perspex, which they picked up and held across the gap from the open roller door.

The first man finally spoke. 'Yep, it fits. I'll attach it to the door jamb tomorrow afternoon with some screws. They won't get in but can still see us loading the frames.' The second man smiled. 'I told you it would work.' The men put the sheet back into the box and left the storeroom.

Rose carefully stepped out from their hiding place. 'I think we've just been introduced to Sneezy and Sleepy.'

They headed back to the bin containing the broken box. 'Give me a hand. We need to solve a giant wooden jigsaw puzzle.' Rose collected the scrap wood in a garbage bag, and they headed to Nic's place to put it all back together. Sandy hefted the bag over her shoulder and broke into song. *'Hey-Ho, Hey-Ho, it's off to Nic's castle we go....'*

Nic strolled into the apartment about an hour later and noticed the pieces of the broken crate on the floor. It was in about thirty pieces, and the women had moved the dining table out of the way to make space. 'I see you've decided to make a mess in my house; thanks for that. Oh, and how did you stop the robot vacuum from coming out and cleaning it up?'

Sandy nodded. 'We opened your bedroom door and threw in a packet of confetti. It's going berserk and must be exhausted by now.'

Nic stood up quickly and headed toward the bedroom. 'Seriously? How long ago was that? The troll must be going wild with all the noise.'

Sandy smiled. 'Oh, about ten minutes. We even asked the troll if it was OK, and as he didn't respond, we assumed it was.'

Nic swung open the bedroom door, but the room was void of the little vacuum unit and silent. 'What did you do with them?'

Rose continued with the banter. 'We flipped it over, and its poor little brush feet kept spinning. It was like wrangling a recalcitrant tortoise, so we stuffed it back into its cupboard, told it to stay, and eventually went quiet. Then we put your stupid coffee maker in with it so it wouldn't be lonely.'

Nic looked at the vacant space in the kitchen, and the machine had indeed been moved. 'Damn, you guys. I need a coffee.'

'You drink Chai Tea, Nic.'

'Oh yeah, I forgot.'

They all turned to look at the pieces on the floor. 'How long have we got to put this thing together before we give it up?'

'Well, we can do it the hard way or the easy way. Which way would you prefer?'

Rose nodded. 'What's the easy way?'

Nic powered up his computer. 'Chewy had me take a 3-D photograph of a random crate just in case we need it for something, and hey presto, it looks like we do.' Sandy looked at the pile of splintered wood. 'So, how does that help?'

Nic continued. 'Well, I take little pictures of all the little pieces and send them to Chewy. He runs a little jigsaw program over it, and it shows us what fits where. It's about ninety per cent effective, and the rest is up to us.'

'That's called cheating.'

'Yep, and it all depends on how many wines we have while waiting.'

Nic moved forward and started taking pictures. The larger pieces were sorted, smaller ones flattened out, a few dead bugs were picked out, half a carrot, and then he straightened up. 'Wow, that was harder than I thought; now I know how Annie Leibowitz felt.' Nic went to bite on the carrot, and Rose slapped it from his hands. 'You don't know who's been nibbling on that. It could have been a rat, and you could get rabies.'

Nic looked at her. 'Rats don't give you rabies. You're more likely to catch it from a bat; it's no wonder I don't play cricket or baseball.'

Wines were poured when the pizza delivery arrived, and they moved outside to the balcony area for the meal. Nic's apartment overlooks the Brisbane River, and they could see across to the other side where the thieves had landed earlier today.

Sandy took a sip of wine and rested against the balcony rail. 'I'd say they were well organised and it would have taken time to put this all together.'

Rose moved over to enjoy the view. 'Nope, I think it was more likely spontaneous. The little boat was stolen and left on the river bank. They only took one painting but could've taken more. It was a deliberate decision to take that one, and it wasn't even the most valuable picture.'

Nic nodded. 'It'll take a couple of weeks to turn up a Pawn Shop or on the internet, so I'll get Chewy to run one of his computer visual things on all painting sites just in case.' Rose turned back to him. 'I think this is more of an inside job.'

Sandy looked at them. 'But why would you steal that specific painting?'

Rose smiled. 'Let me think. How about someone who loves Hawaiian sunsets and misses the Big Kahuna back home?'

Nic raised some of his observations. 'Well, the guy did use a full Spiderman suit, with a full head mask, so no face to match and no hair to see. Nothing but Spidey head to toe. I overheard some witnesses talking about the heist, and some said it was the real Aquaman driving the boat. Some even said it was actually Jason Momoa himself.'

'Wasn't he the guy that played Drogo in Games of Thrones?'

Nic nodded. 'Yep.'

Rose added. 'I'm slowly watching that series on Netflix. It seems to drag on.'

Nic looked at her. 'Seriously...and you think my Dad jokes are bad?' Rose shrugged her shoulders. 'Well, what do we do now? It's getting late, and Chewy hasn't returned with the jigsaw thing yet. We'll go home and prepare for the big day tomorrow.'

Nic nodded. 'Yep, if anything turns up from Chewy, I'll make a start. The main scam event will be tomorrow, before, during or after the show. I don't know which yet.'

Rose and Sandy were back at the Museum site early the following day at her Father's insistence. Zachariah had rung late in the evening and demanded they put together a brief regarding the theft of the painting and how much he was expected to lose now that the Hawaiian pieces had been removed from the auction.

Rose handed over a quickly prepared summary of the estimated impact and stood in the reception building where the 'fake' paintings had been hung. There were already prospective buyers in the room. Zachariah flicked through the portfolio. 'Well, Rosemary, this is quite impressive. I'm surprised how quickly you put this together; it is very detailed. I'm not quite sure why you refer to unknown suspects, though. Do you think I'm not in control?'

Rose responded. 'I would prefer that we don't discuss it here, however, yes, I'm concerned that something untoward is about to happen here today. It's just a feeling I have. Let us move into an office to discuss it.' Zachariah shook his head. 'Nope, let's have it out right here.' He lowered his voice. 'Young lady, there is nothing you need to be concerned with. I've had a quiet moment with the two colleagues who will catalogue the sales and crate them for shipment. They are not concerned, and neither should you be.'

Rose looked at him. 'I'm concerned for your reputation, Father. If this is more than what it appears, it's only your name on everything. Like the site lease, the registration of the company name, and the delivery consignments.'

He glared at her. 'Yes, I'm fully aware of that. I'm also the Sole Director and Shareholder of several companies. Why is this one of concern?'

'Father, I know you didn't register the name 'It Keeps Changing'; it's not your style. The business address is registered to your home and not your business, so don't you think that's suspicious? How many of your companies have your address listed?'

'Young lady, I don't know what or why you think this is.' Jana overheard the comment and interjected. 'What's going on, Father?'

Rose took a deep breath. 'Well, Mother, I have a distinct impression that the whole art show is a sham, and there seemed to be several other people involved here. Besides that, there is much more. None of the artwork has been insured in situ, which I think contravenes Auction conditions. I can't find anyone else's name or anything related to the sale apart from the QR link back to the artist, and as for your five colleagues, we've resorted to calling them.'

Nic had finally arrived, moved into earshot, and managed to catch Rose's eye, so she stopped talking and Jana continued: 'I think we've heard enough, Rosemary. You have never wanted to be involved in Father's business interests, and now, because you have been roaming around with your friend Nic Thorn, you think you have the right to insult your Father.' Sandy took hold of Rose's arm and tried to move her. 'Rose let's take a better look at those packing crates. There's plenty in the shed.' Rose chose not to continue, and they moved away, leaving her Father furious.

'I have not finished with you yet, young lady. I forbid you to look at anything more.'

Rose turned and held up her forefinger to make her point. 'I'll say this once, Father. Regardless of what happens or doesn't happen here, I'll not stand by and watch. There's something is not right quite here. I will get to the bottom of it.'

Rose and Sandy moved outside, then a moment later, where Nic joined them and saw Rose was still seething. 'That was a little .... intense. I don't like it when the children are fighting.'

Rose took a deep breath. 'Well, tell me I'm wrong, Nic.'

'I can't yet, but we'll know in a few hours.'

CHAPTER 21

It was just before 2 p.m., The Pining Parrots had stopped playing, and the crowds were gathered around the tents waiting for the show to begin. Zachariah shook everyone's hand, thanking them for attending and finally moved to a vacant space: 'Ladies and gentlemen, boys and girls, artists, and buyers; welcome to the Brisbane Maritime Museum's inaugural Art event. I know this is the first year of many more. You do not have to be registered; the piece will be yours upon the hammer's fall. My colleague and friend, Michael Bush, will be the Master of Ceremonies. We will start precisely at the stroke of two.' Michael moved up to Zachariah. There was back-slapping and exaggerated double-handshaking. Rose looked around for support from Nic but saw him slip into the storage shed via a side door. *Damn you, Nic, just what are you up to?'*

Michael had now taken the front position: 'Hello, Ladies and Gentlemen. Yes, my name is Michael Bush, and for those who don't know me, I am related to George W. and his son, POTUS. God Bless the US of A. For those who know me, I am not related to George Bush, but I'm still trying to get them to adopt me.' There was a murmur of laughter, and he continued. 'You have noticed that we have now put tickets on the art pieces. This is the minimum we expect to achieve. It's like a silent auction with words. You can cross it out and add your number, so the highest number at the end will win the piece. Please leave the painting where it is as we'll have people gather them and place them into their specially made wooden shipping box.'

Zachariah nodded, then stepped in. 'Please remember, it is not an auction per se. We will not be taking bids and scaring people out of taking the opportunity to purchase. You will be allowed three minutes to enter the tent, and we will close down the flaps on all four sides so you can make your offer privately. You have been given numbered tickets, and this relates to your offer. We will announce who has been successful once the paintings have been crated up, and you will collect them from the work shed.'

Rose leaned into Sandy. 'I wonder what happens if someone marks up all the paintings to raise the price and then doesn't pay for it.'

Sandy nodded. 'I wondered that too, and wasn't George H the Father and George W the son?'

'Yes, and yet Michael still carries that stupid joke fifteen years later.'

The show began: The first group came up and was herded through the tent, but only five entered. It took less than ten minutes and was the same process for the next tent, too, but fortunately, there were at least seven prospective buyers in this case. Rose sensed her father getting nervous, and as they moved to the next tent, only two people were waiting for access.

Sandy tapped Rose on the shoulder and oversaw Michael enter the first tent. 'Surely the scam is not that simple. Your Father sends Michael into the tent to mark up the price?'

Rose shook her head. 'Nope. That won't work, as the buyers will deny it's their writing.'

Sandy nodded. 'OK, but have you seen Nic? The band has stopped playing, and he's not with them.'

Rose continued. 'He snuck into the work shed. I expect he's closer to sorting this out than we are. He's been doing it a bit longer than us, but it's very nerve-racking when it's so close to home. I hope my Father knows what he's doing. The more we have to do with these scams, the closer we get to the sun and sooner or later, we'll melt our wings.'

Sandy nodded. 'What do we do now?'

'We wait.'

The prospective buyers completed the inspection on all five tents and were milling around, waiting for the next event. Michael had also managed to scope out all the tents and stood beside Zachariah.

They were both smiling and then Michael approached Rose and Sandy. 'Well, well, well, look who turned up. Your Father's told me about that little charade with the little portfolio thing, and your concern for his reputation is quite....um... laughable.'

Rose defensively crossed her arms over her chest. 'Did you mark any prices when you were in the tents then, Michael?'

He looked at her sternly. 'It is none of your business, but I obey your Father.'

Rose glared at him. 'I hope he keeps you on a long leash.'

Sandy stopped her. 'He's not worth it.'

Michael leered at her. 'Oh, I'm so worth it, Sandy, but you'll never know.'

Rose shook her head. 'Michael, please leave us alone. I assume you'll be standing by my Father's side when this goes south?'

'I think you mean *if* it goes south, not when. Your Father has done a wonderful thing with the Art Show and Shine. It brings so much joy to many people's otherwise humdrum lives.'

'It's a scam, Michael. We haven't worked out how yet, but it's a scam. How else do you explain why someone would steal their painting from the exhibition?'

Michael looked at her. 'What are you on about now?'

'The Spiderman guy. It was his painting. He stole it so it wouldn't get tarnished by whatever happened here. When I helped his mother load the rest of her paintings into her truck, I found the costume hidden behind a sliding panel at the back of the van.

'So what?'

'Well, he was expecting around twenty thousand for it, but somehow it got pulled from the auction?'

'How do you know he didn't arrange with your Father, and it was all part of the drama of the show?'

Rose looked at him sternly. 'Really? Are you going for collusion? I don't think my Father would be up to that. Besides, all he could talk about was the loss of commission on her painting sales. He's not that savvy.'

'Oh, he's very savvy, and I ought to know. I'm his Accountant.'

'Please leave, Michael. We've got to sort out what is going on here.'

Michael headed back to Zachariah with one last quip. 'Do not follow this up, Rosemary. You do not know who you are dealing with.'

Sandy gathered Rose's arm and headed towards the storage shed. 'I didn't know you saw the Spidey costume in the van.'

'I didn't.'

All the paintings had now been gathered from the tents and were being collated for shipping. A crowd stood before the Perspex sheet that had now been secured across the door. The sheet obscured half of the view into the shed, and two men were putting the paintings into their allocated crates. Those pieces that were sold had been appropriately marked by the two men. Each was numbered with the corresponding winning bid. Rose knew Nic was still in the shed but didn't know why or where. Zachariah was now inside the shed holding a mobile EFTPOS machine in readiness for the sale process to begin.

He called everyone to attention: 'Thank you, ladies and gentlemen. I'll read out the winning ticket, then the bidder can meet me to pay.'

Rose was still trying to figure out how it could be a scam, and as everything started to seem more legitimate, she felt relieved.

The two men stepped onto a wooden platform, and a much larger wooden crate was now underneath them. It was about three metres by three metres square.

Rose pulled out her phone. 'Smile, Father. Please let me take your picture.'

Her Father reluctantly complied and continued: 'My two gentlemen will place your paintings into their shipping crates. It will happen right before you. The crate will then be sealed for your protection. You cannot open the crate until you log in via the QR code. A secure password will then be sent to your mobile phone. Please open the crate carefully, as we will not be liable for any damage during transit or the crate's opening.' He paused for effect. 'Let's begin.... Number 'One Twenty.''

A woman held her ticket up. 'That's me.'

One of the men was standing atop the large box, and the second man handed up the winning art piece. The man held the painting by the side panels, raised it above his head and carefully slid it into the shipping crate. It was a very theatrical performance. He then handed the crate back to his partner and took a step backward to wait for the next instruction, and then Zachariah completed his part of the transaction.

It was a relatively simple process. The woman was handed the shipping container and moved away.

'Next.... Number five.' A man nodded, and they went through the same process.

Rose continued to take photos and noticed each time the man standing on top of the box made a small step backwards.

After about an hour, most of the paintings and crates had now been exchanged, and the box man nodded to Zachariah:

'Ladies and Gentlemen, we'll be taking a small break now. Please bear with us.'

By this time, only about thirteen remained, so Zachariah moved to the side of the store room to exit by a side door, pressed a controller and the door slowly closed.

Sandy had been observing the two box men and leaned towards Rose. 'I can't see how this is a scam.'

Rose nodded. 'It looks like they're sliding the painting frame through the middle panel so I assume there must be hinges on the bottom of the crates. Also, have you noticed the guy standing on top of the box? He keeps stepping backwards.'

After a small talk with the remaining buyers, Zachariah announced they would restart, so he pressed the controller and raised the door.

The two men were again standing on either side of a crate, and this time, Zachariah stayed outside the storeroom. 'There's only a few left now, so I'll stay here until we finish. It's a little bit small with three of us in there.'

Rose whispered to Sandy. 'Four, I hope.'

The box man again jumped up atop the box and waited for the next number to be called, and the process started again until there was one painting left. Zachariah clasped his hands: 'Ladies and gentlemen, we are down to the last purchase. I am very pleased to announce it sold for a resounding seventy thousand dollars. Would the bidder for number Twenty-Five please come forward?'

The crowd looked around, and then Michael stepped out. 'That's me.'

Rose shook her head. 'And that's how they bring up the sales average.'

Sandy looked at her. 'Say what?'

Rose continued. 'Well, it's all about the numbers. My Father is a numbers guy. Let's say you sell ten paintings at a hundred dollars each, which puts the average at a hundred dollars. In this case, the paintings have sold for an average of twenty thousand, with the lowest at eight thousand. Suddenly, the highest bid is seventy thousand, and Bazinga, the average has just been increased by around five grand.'

Sandy shook her head. 'So that's the scam? The average sales so your Father can leverage from that for the next exhibition?'

Rose thought about it. 'Nope, it can't be. That's too obvious.'

'So, what then?'

'I have no idea, but I think it all hinges on the hinges....'

CHAPTER 22

The last sale had been finalised, the Perspex sheet removed, and the two men moved to a small truck parked nearby. They used a forklift to load the box they had been standing on during the sale process, and from the glares and stares, nothing or no one would dare get in their way. Everyone accepted they were tidying up. The truck's rear door was secured, the two men clambered in, and it slowly chugged through double exit gates to exit the Museum site.

Rose and Sandy watched it drive away, then moved towards the band as they prepared to restart. They sat in front of the performers and realised Nic wasn't there. Carly moved up to them. 'Have you guys seen Nic? We have to play for the next fifteen minutes whilst everyone finishes up. I rang his mobile, but it must be turned off.'

Rose nodded. 'That's OK; I'm sure you'll manage. He'll turn up eventually. I'll ring Chewy and get him to ping Nic's phone if he doesn't. It's got a locater in it.'

Carly took a step towards the band, then hesitated. 'Can either of you play a stand-up bass?'

Rose laughed, and Sandy looked at her. 'Hey, I'm only a singer, so it's up to you, Rose.' Rose looked around one last time. 'Damn you, Nic,' then she moved to the double bass and held it towards her. 'Ok, I'll do it, but I'll only pluck the strings. I won't use the bowie thing.'

Sticks Out strolled over. 'Don't worry about it. I'll put a piece of duct tape across the top of the neck so anything you play won't be heard. We'll rely on the back-track.'

'That's cheating the audience.'

'Hey, if it's good enough for The Strolling Bones, I'm sure we can be forgiven; after all, those guys are over eighty.'

'They don't use a back-track.'

'Nope, they just use a whole eight-piece backup band.'

The Pining Parrots re-started with a reprise of 'Bridge over Troubled Water', and the remaining crowd was not at all concerned that the band, having played the song two days before, had opened with the sound of a solemn and sultry bow. Rose was enjoying the experience and was a little disappointed when Carly announced their last song. It was the song written by Don McLean dedicated to Vicent Van Gogh. The song finished, the audience clapped, and the band started to pack up.

Nic was still not around, so Rose and Sandy said their goodbyes to the band members and decided to return to Nic's apartment to wait for him.

They had managed to avoid Zachariah, Jana, and Michael, having exited the exhibition hall. Rose noticed her Father's 'Lavender Bay' print had a sold sticker on it and paused by Uncle Albert's painting to join the small crowd surrounding the piece.

Someone was taking a very close interest in it, then the man stepped back and declared to no one in particular. 'This one has genuine craquelure.'

Sandy scrambled to look up the word's meaning on her phone, then showed it to Rose: *The craquelure is like a painting's fingerprint: different images from other countries, produced at different times, have different craquelure patterns, and they are tough to replicate in a fake...*

The man 'Googled' the artist's name and blew a loud whistle. 'I think this is real. Who owns it? Does anyone know if it is for sale?'

Rose and Sandy ignored him, but unfortunately, Zachariah hadn't and duly declared: 'It's mine.' The man immediately approached Zachariah. 'I will pay you one hundred thousand dollars cash right now.'

Rose tapped her Father on the shoulder. 'It's not for sale, Father.' Her Father ignored her, and the interested man continued to press his quest. 'Sir, I am a Professor of Modern Art here in Brisbane, and this piece should be in a Museum. Not on a wall...in here.'

Rose felt a presence close to her and turned; it was Nic. He whispered, 'Ask the Professor about the painting purported to be by the same artist hanging in the Gallery of Modern Art in Sydney, New South Wales.'

Rose smiled. 'Sorry, Professor, I was in Sydney recently and saw a similar painting in a gallery. Is it by the same artist?'

The man's expression turned a little dour. 'Well, yes, but that one is not the same.'

Nic whispered again. 'Ask him about the controversy.'

The man overheard the word. 'I know, I know. The one in Sydney has been declared not having been painted by the Master, rather one of his students, and is not signed. I will up my offer to three hundred thousand.'

Michael was jockeying for a better position to add his opinion. 'You cannot prove it is yours, Rose. I was at the will reading. It could be challenged that Albert had bequeathed the piece to your Father.'

Zachariah clasped his hands together. 'Thank you, Michael.'

Sandy looked at Rose. 'I don't think we can win this.'

Nic smiled. 'But I can. Ask them to take it off the wall and check out the back of the frame.'

Zachariah overheard this time. 'What is it any business of yours, Mr Thorn.'

'It's something called transfer of ownership, Zachariah. It's only a minor issue, but I'm sure we can sort it out right now if you care to remove the black felt from the back of the picture, as there's a nice little letter of declaration that you might like to read.' Michael removed the painting, placed it faced down on a nearby table and carefully peeled back one corner of the black felt. It revealed an old envelope:

'*To Sandra Fraser and Rosemary Palmer. My Best Friends.*'

Zachariah quickly gathered the envelope and lifted open the flap. It contained a single sheet of paper, and he read it out loud:

To my favourite ladies.

Thank you for everything. This is my final gift to you both. I hope you still miss me as much as I do you. God Bless. Until we meet again.

Yours sincerely, Charles Albert Brown – Uncle Albert.

The document had been notarised, and the signature witnessed by the Governor General of Queensland. Some of the crowd 'Oohed' and one woman began to cry. Nic leaned into Zachariah. 'I told you so.'

Jana called out. 'It's a fake. Father, you have nothing to worry about. I bet this is another one of those Nic Thorn scams.'

Nic shook his head. 'Sorry, Jana, it's too high brow for me, but don't you just hate it when the witness was available today to confirm that she witnessed the declaration?' An elegant woman stepped forward from the gathered crowd. 'Yes, that is my signature, and the transfer of ownership is legitimate. Congratulations, Rose and Sandy.'

Rose and Sandy left the astonished crowd, a frustrated Michael, a very annoyed Queensland Museum official, and Rose's parents in their wake.

Nic arrived at his apartment about an hour later to join Rose and Sandy, and they sat down to enjoy some sandwiches. 'Thanks for joining the band at such short notice. Did you miss me?'

Rose looked at him. 'Well, it's hard to investigate as a team when there's one that's gone AWOL. There's no 'I' in team, Nic.'

'Nope, but I had things to do. Like viewing the vision from the Ferry people, hiding from the scammers, and solving the mystery of the lost painting. Oh, and thanking the Governor for finding the time to attend to the witnessing of the unveiling of your newly found bequest. Thank you, by the way, as you are the genuine owners of a piece of art allegedly worth over four hundred thousand dollars.'

Rose ignored his last comment. 'Well, did the ferry vision show anything?'

'Yep, they gave me a lovely compilation CD showing the view from two ferries. I'll play it for you, but there's no music.' Nic loaded the disc into his computer and linked up the feed. 'Apparently, there's nothing much here, but we see the two guys dump the boat and scamper away. It's still interesting to see a real Spiderman and Aqua-man do their thing.' The view lasted about ten minutes.

Rose looked at him. 'OK, it's the son then. Don't you agree?'

'Yep.'

Sandy looked at them. 'So what did you see? I saw Spidey and a squidgy Aqua-man jumping out of a boat carrying a painting held in a waterproof pouch.'

Rose asked Nic to replay the vision of the men stepping off the boat. '*There.*'

Sandy nodded. 'What are we looking at?'

'When the guys looked at each other, they do that Hawaiian hand signal thing.'

Nic nodded. 'A bit of a leap, even for Spidey, but there is also the fact that we found a Spiderman suit stuffed into one of the lockers at the University Swimming Pool, and we have the camera view of two men heading towards Comic-Con just after the heist.'

'So?'

'Well, one was still dressed as squidgy Aqua-man and the other is dressed as a guy from Hawaii who was previously dressed as Spiderman, who's just stolen his painting from the Art Show and Shine.'

Rose looked at Nic. 'That will probably do it. Anything else?'

'Well, when we caught up with them, he confessed to stealing the painting.'

'That will work too. Did he say why he stole it?'

'Yep. He thought the auction was a sham and didn't want to be a part of it.'

'Did he tell you why and how?'

'Nope.'

'So, is he being charged with theft?'

'I don't think so, as you can't be charged with stealing your artwork.'

Rose looked at him. 'Damn you, Nic.'

'Why this time?'

'Well, it means my Father *is* most likely involved, and by the way, where's your phone?'

Nic pulled a phone from his pocket. 'This one?'

Rose shook her head. 'Nope, the other one I pulled from your tight wetsuit the other night.'

'Oh, you remember that?'

'Yes, it was a mini that caused me to have a maxi anxiety attack having to get so close to you.'

Nic smiled, then tapped an app on his phone. It revealed a locator 'ping'.

'By the looks of it, my other phone is just across the New South Wales border.'

'So, you're tracking the truck? Whose? Mrs White's and Dopey, or Sleepy and Sneezy's?'

'The one with the stolen art in it.'

Sandy took another sip of her wine, then sighed 'So, tell us about the elephant in the room then.'

'Which one? The elephant that forgot to tell you about a precious painting found inside a box left in the back of a car in a storage shed, or the elephant

that worked out how the painting scam was put together?' Nic smiled, then added. 'I'm both the ele-
phants, by the way.'

Rose sat back down. 'I don't think we want to
know about the painting, so tell us about the scam.
Is my Father involved?'

Nic took a bite of the sandwich, then held his
finger up, so they had to wait for his response.
Rose noted the delay. 'Tough question?'

'Nope, tough roast beef, and well, the short answer is no. I spent the afternoon hanging from the
rafters in the storage shed, and just so you know,
being a bat isn't all it's cut out to be, Anyway, it was
very clever, one of the best cut-and-shuts I've seen
for a while.'

Rose opened her phone, started scrolling
through the photos she'd taken during the auction,
and stopped at one. 'You know, I wondered whose
leg was hanging from the ceiling.'

Sandy joined Rose, and they expanded the vision on the screen. 'It's quite a feat to hang up
there for so long. I hope the possums didn't bite.'

Nic nodded. 'No possums, but thanks for asking.
I was pretty uncomfortable until I realised what
the two men were doing. It was all about a strip
of hinges they had built into the crates.' Nic stood
up, moved over to the windows of his apartment,
and ran his hand along the plantation shutters.
Rose and Sandy watched as he slid them open and
closed with the movement of his hand.

Nic continued: 'They took the first painting and loaded it into the crate, '*nothing to see here*', but when the guy on top took a step backwards they lifted the next painting on top. He then opened a hinge plate under his foot.' Nic pushed the plantation shutter into an open position. 'Whilst the first guy unscrewed the little hooks on the frame, the second guy released the hinge on the bottom of the crate, so when the guy standing on the box held it up and aligned the frame, it simply dropped into the larger wooden crate they were standing on.'

Rose smiled. 'That's a lot of planning.'

'Yep, and they still had to get the box out of the Museum, but no one stopped them. Where was Superman when you needed him? We could have used his X-ray vision.'

Sandy looked at them. 'Small hole in the plan, apart from what I assume, they might have used a lead-lined box just in case Superman turned up, didn't anyone notice their crates didn't contain a painting? What happened when they opened it?'

'It was all about the weight. A wooden crate with or without the frame would weigh much the same, and they've had a plan to cover off the opening of the crate too.'

Rose nodded. 'Yes, my Father told the buyers to wait for the password to be sent. The QR code is the gate, but the password is the key. Otherwise, they'll have to smash the box to access the art piece.'

'Yep, so I would say about now your Father is getting calls as the passwords haven't been sent yet.'

Rose was about to respond when her phone rang. It was her Father.

'Hello, Father. I assume you want to speak to Nic?' Rose handed her phone to Nic. 'Hello, Zachariah. I assume your clients are trying to get into their paintings and can't open the crates?'

'Yes, Mr Thorn and I want to know what you will do about it.'

Nic smiled. 'If you allow me the indulgence, Zachariah, I must make several phone calls. I'll call you back in half an hour.'

Nic stood up and took a sip of wine. 'Please excuse me, ladies. I must make a call.' They waited for him to move inside or at least out of earshot. However, he moved towards the balcony instead.

Rose looked at Sandy. 'I hate it when he does that.'

'Me too. I don't want to know or need to know what he knows.'

CHAPTER 23

Mrs White and Dopey were about three hours into their drive to Melbourne when Dopey looked over at his Mother. 'The heist was so cool, and thanks for putting it all together. Where did you find Aqua-Man, though? He was quite a chatterbox.'

'I put an ad up on Facebook.'

Dopey laughed. 'You know I confessed, don't you?'

'Yes, but don't worry, I think it was the right thing to do. Those two guys running the show gave me the creeps.'

'Who? Michael Bush and Zachariah Palmer?'

'No, the two guys putting the crates together. I reckon they were up to something, but don't worry, we'll sell our stuff in Melbourne. The gallery has given us the first Tuesday in November for the exhibition. Apparently, there is a horse race on the same day, but not many people attend it.' They pulled into a Petrol Station and could hear a phone ringing...

After about two hours of driving, Sleepy and Sneezy pulled their little truck into the 'Elements Resort at Byron Bay. They had booked into their rooms and were collecting their luggage from their van when they heard a phone ringing. They looked at each other. 'You dope, you've dropped your phone.'

The younger man pulled his phone from his pocket. 'It's not mine.' They scrambled to find where it was ringing from and decided it was coming from the wooden boxes in the back of the van. The phone stopped ringing...

Back in Brisbane, Nic redialled, but this time, it was answered: 'Hello, this is Nic Thorn, and I believe you are transporting a stolen painting.'

'I'm sorry, Mr Thorn, but you can't charge someone for stealing their painting. You know I confessed as you were there.'

Nic looked over to Rose and Sandy. 'That's true, but you can be charged pretending you're a superhero. That's still against the law in Australia.'

The man hesitated, and Nic continued: 'Anyway. Good luck selling the art in Melbourne, and please avoid the first Tuesday in November for your exhibition despite what they promise you. The whole state of Victoria stops for a horse race. Enjoy the rest of your stay in Australia, and let me know if you need anything.' Nic hung up. 'And now for the call that I have to make.'

He dialled again, and this time the phone was answered. 'Hello, this is Nic Thorn, and I know you are transporting stolen paintings. Please do not move from your current whereabouts. The Police have been notified.' He looked over to Rose and Sandy, and they both responded. 'Damn you, Nic.'

The call was disconnected, and Nic called Zachariah. 'Rose has recovered the stolen paintings.' Rose stood up, went over to him and they hugged. 'Thanks, Nic, another scam busted by Nic Thorn and Associates, and this time it *was* personal.'

An hour later, they were finalising the brief to be presented to the Police when Nic's doorbell chimed. *'Delivery for Nic Thorn at the foyer.'* Nic left the apartment and, about five minutes returned with one metre by one-metre square wooden crate. Rose looked at it. 'Another recovered stolen painting?'

'Not quite.'

Nic located a screwdriver from his utility drawer, popped open the lid and the box was filled with wooden shredding. Nic brushed the shavings aside, revealing the shoulders and back of a marble statue. 'It's something a friend of mine was working on.'

Sandy peered into the box. 'Is it a replica of Michelangelo's David?'

'Nup.' Nic removed the Styrofoam residue, and the whole statue was finally visible. It was a nude sculpture, from a rearview, at least. Rose and Sandy were now very interested. Rose smiled. 'So, it is supposed to be you? And a replica of David? And ...what about the front view...and the ....'

'Toe?'

Nic smiled. 'Yep, let's call it the toe.'

Nic reached into the box, collected the piece by the waist, fully extracted it and managed to face it away from them, but they insisted he turn it around. 'OK, guys, close your eyes and don't peek until I tell you to.'

Rose and Sandy laughed, then reluctantly complied, so Nic turned the sculpture to face them. 'It's a full frontal nude, so please be ready. Now.'

The women turned and then opened their eyes. It *was* a full frontal nude, but a tiny marble apron covered the nether regions. Nic shrugged. 'It was the middle of winter, and there wasn't a heater when I posed for it.' Nic was about to make another excuse when his phone rang. 'This is Nic Thorn.' Nic put the phone on speaker: 'Thank you, Mr Thorn. We've recovered the paintings and made the arrests. It's all very simple. Do you want to meet us down here and collect the paintings?'

'At Byron Bay?'

'Yes, the surf is up now, so it's quite busy, and Thor is in town too.'

Sandy looked at him and nodded. 'We'll be in for that. Anytime we can glimpse a Hemsworth, it makes a trip to Byron worthwhile.'

Rose nodded. 'And the surfs up, which means all's well that ends swell.'

Nic looked at her and shook his head. 'That is so bad, Rose.'

Sandy smiled and began reviewing the completed computer compilation of the smashed box jigsaw. 'I get it now. There were hinges on the bottom of each of the wooden crates, and as the guy standing atop the box made a step backwards he opened a panel with his foot and the art piece slipped straight through into the crate below, as you said Rose, it hinged on the hinges.'

Rose nodded. 'Quite a good plan, but we framed them in the end.'

Nic shook his head again. 'Please stop with the Dad jokes, Rose.'

A few weeks later, the group had made their way back to Brisbane and were gathered in the foyer of the Gallery of Modern Art at Southbank. Rose had asked her Father and Mother to meet them there and they insisted on bringing Michael, Dimond and the children. Rose accepted on the proviso that they all behave.

Around forty others had now joined them and the crowd was led upstairs to a private viewing room, and it looked like a Pied Piper of Paintings was in town and congregated in the small space that housed one single piece of art. It was shrouded in a velvet cloth.

Rose turned to address the crowd: 'For those that don't know, Sandy and I recently uncovered a painting and selling scam at the Maritime Museum. All the paintings were recovered, but we are here to unveil a painting discovered during the investigation.'

A murmur of anticipation covered the room when Rose and Sandy approached each side of the hanging and gathered the side ropes. Sandy took over: 'It was recently discovered there were two versions of the same art piece. The artist did not paint the one hanging at the Gallery of Modern Art in Sydney, but rather his student.'

Rose and Sandy pulled on the ropes, and the shroud dropped to the floor: 'Ladies and Gentlemen, this is the original. It was thought to have been lost. However, it was recently recovered in the back of a car that had been in storage for three years.' The crowd gasped, and Rose continued. 'This piece has been generously donated to the Gallery of Modern Art here in Brisbane by the benefactors of the estate of Charles Albert Brown, our Uncle Albert.'

Nic nodded, then whispered. 'Nice,' and hugged them both.

Rose and Sandy manage to hold back their tears.

Meantime, Zachariah and Michael were dumbstruck as they both realised they'd lost access to well over four hundred thousand dollars worth of inheritance despite having no actual entitlement. Michael abruptly moved towards them, but someone else sensed his reaction as they managed to stop him mid-stride:

'Hello, Michael Bush. My name is Gordon Tracey, and I represent the Australian Taxation Office in Brisbane. I am here to personally let you know that we are about to commence an audit of your Accounting Firm. Please ensure everything is made available to my team..'

The man paused for effect. 'And we start tomorrow....'

Dedication

Thanks to Don McLean for providing the words of Vincent (Vinnie to his friends).

(Rose, Vinnie was from the 70's TV show Welcome Back Kotter)

(No, Nic, it was Vincent Van Gogh. Have you heard of him?)

Introducing Book 7 in the series:

Seven Hapless Hoops

Rosemary Palmer was standing in the middle of a manure-filled horse stable, chewing on the end of a bent straw, but unfortunately, it wasn't attached to the side of a margarita glass. Rose spat it out, sighed heavily, and rested her chin on the handle of a rake. 'Damn it, Sandy, this stuff stinks.'

Her BFF, Sandy Fraser, had just scooped the last shovel full and placed it carefully into a wheelbarrow. 'I know, and I still can't believe what we must do to get a dollar in our pockets. Life is too short for this type of crappy job.'

Rose was about to respond when their scam-busting associate and friend, Nic Thorn, ambled towards them formally dressed in a 'Brisbane - Doomben Horse Racing Course' uniform. 'How long do we have to keep doing this, Nic?'

'Until it's done...then you can start in the next stable.'

Sandy looked at him. 'You're joking?'

'Nope...if I were joking, I would have said a horse walks into a bar, and the barman says, why the long face.'

Rose leaned down, gathered a clump of soggy manure, and threw it at him, but Nic managed to evade the incoming missile, however, the man standing behind him bore the brunt of the lump instead. The man was wearing a white suit, a matching white trilby, leaning on a beechwood cane with a gold ferrule. The man frowned and removed his hat. 'I guess I should introduce myself then. My name is Charles Carrington, The Third, and I'm the President of K.P.I Events.'

Rose collected a bucket of water and a sponge, then began to wipe the residue from the man's suit with her hands, but as she moved lower down his torso, he quickly grabbed her wrist. 'Sorry, Ms Palmer, I can't let you do that.' Rose stopped, looked at him, and he added: 'The water is icy cold, it will make the suit shrink.'

Nic stepped into the stable, gathered the rake and Rose's hand, and led her from the cemented pen. Rose brushed herself down. 'Have we finished yet?'

Nic nodded. 'Yep, but you'll need to move as the horse is coming back.' Sandy and Rose stepped aside as the strapper led the horse into the stable. Sandy patted the rear flank of the magnificent animal. 'What's the horse's name?'

The strapper began brushing down the animal. 'No name.'

Rose nodded. 'That's so sad…I thought every horse had to have a name. It forms part of the lineage.' The strapper stopped mid-stroke, then nodded towards the lintel across the top of the pen. Rose and Sandy looked towards the wooden nameplate. It read: **'No Neighm.'**

Nic tapped the nameplate. 'Yep, this is a Horse with No Neighm.'

For more reading:

<u>One Tricked Phoney</u>

Rose needed a +1, but not for the usual wedding/party. She was going to a funeral and needed a quiet, unassuming type. The best option was to use her dating site, but when Nic Thorn arrived, he was anything but a wallflower. Nic coerces them into his madcap investigations of scams, frauds, and misunderstandings. These modern-day adventures lead them from one lively caper to another, involving portrait provenance, invoice inaccuracy, and a recycler's relapse, on their travels from Brisbane, Adelaide, to the SA border.

<u>Two Hurtled Gloves</u>

Nic has to investigate a wedded miss, the misguided pretence of Tasmanian Tiger tracking, and some banking bastardry. Rose was to be a bride again, but this time, Nic Thorn ensured it wasn't the short, fat, and shallow man her parents forced her to marry the first time around. Then they move on to another tale, this one tracking down the elusive and believed to be extinct Thylacine. Nic finally introduces them to the peaceful banking world, however, much more is involved when the loan arranger is unmasked as a fraud and he isn't banking on getting caught.

<u>Three French Bens</u>

Nic's friend, Benoit Trudeau, is one-third of the 'Three French Bens'. He has just bought into a high-end restaurant, so he called Nic's Team in to have a look, as the numbers look fishy, and they might have to go angling for the truth. Then

Nic and his crew head to Rockhampton to help the Queensland Department of Agriculture look into some cattle duffing, as apparently, it's heard a lot up that way. Finally, Sandy has to deal with an old school friend or is that a fiend lending her at her expense?

Four Brooding Birds

Nic and the team are brought in to investigate reptile smuggling. Lizards have been discovered stuffed into a women's singlet, and her accomplice is caught with his jocks of frogs, but of course, they deny any knowledge of how they got in there. Then the team tries to drink from the sweet success of wines, but this just turns out to be someone who can't stop whining about how he has to keep everything bottled up inside and to complete their subsequent investigation, they have to look into genuine budgie smugglers.

Five Mouldy Bins

It's Christmas in July, and the Department of Health in Brisbane is concerned that someone may be stuffing their mattress with ill-gotten gains, so Nic and the team are brought in to bring it to a head – reindeer style. In the meantime, h their 'friend' Dimond, keeps handing over her hard-earned to lease a new rental property for the family, but the Real Estate Agent only takes the deposit in cash. Then, the team gets involved in a diamond scam but getting stranded in Dubai on the way to South Africa was never in the plan.

Seven Hapless Hoops

One of Nic's old friends calls upon him to locate his missing wife; whilst this is not generally in the scope of what they do, it is too close to home for Nic not to be in the right place to investigate. Meantime, a car vanishes without a trace, and a horse racing scam is gathering pace, but will they be too late to save face?

AUTHOR'S BIOGRAPHY:

The author is a former long-term banker by profession and worked in the Bank's Credit Card Fraud Team, where he obtained a Private Investigators Licence. The author resides between Adelaide, South Australia, and the Sunshine Coast, Queensland. In November 2022, the author won an award from Wakefield Press, Adelaide for his short story: 'Car on a Hill'.

The following Nic Thorn and Associates titles are available for online purchase: One Tricked Phoney, Two Hurtled Gloves, Three French Bens, Four Brooding Birds, Five Mouldy Bins and Six Geezers Lying. To be published in 2025: Seven Hapless Hoops and Eight Dave's are Weak. To be published in 2026: Nine Means Know and Ten Little Idioms.

Other titles written by the author:

Driven to Kill/dp/1763732908
The Flighters – Believe. dp/0975668447